Efland,

 I hope you

this as much as I enjoyed

writing it. Merry Christmas & a

wonderful new year!

Cindy

One Grave
Secret

By Cindy Ponds Newell

One Grave Secret

ISBN-13: 978-1493510009 | ISBN-10: 1493510002

First Paperback Edition
Printed in the United States of America

Editing services provided by Todd Barselow
www.toddedits.com

Formatting services and cover design provided by
Rene Folsom with Phycel Designs
www.phycel.com

Dedication

To my beautiful children:
Hannah, Luke and Grace

To my sister, Tammy Thomas,
and my brother, Michael "Bubba" Ponds

To Dawn, my almost sister and forever best friend,
thank you for helping me so much!

Thank you, Tammy Dean and the "real" Lori
for your help in making this work!

And mostly, to Jesus
Because you see the depths of my heart and you still love me.

Table of Contents

"The boundaries which divide life and death are at best shadowy and vague. Who shall say where the one ends, and where the other begins?"

— Edgar Allen Poe

One Grave Secret

Part One: Lori

One Grave Secret

Prologue

September 25, 1973

Even though it was September, there was no relief from the North Carolina heat in sight. Fall would come, but not this day.

Sweat dropped down on Lori Eades from the ponytail she sported as she waited for her mom to pick her up after school. It wasn't too exciting, but even a trip to Bell's store, called Elco to those who didn't personally know Mr. Bell, was better than nothing.

Lori's mom, Denise, was tired of the drab blue curtains that graced her kitchen windows. They had hung there for four years, and she was ready for a change. Using money she had tucked away, she had decided to go for yellow. Anything to brighten the area and maybe even add some sunshine to the otherwise plain room.

When Lori saw the family car, a brown Buick pull in to the school parking lot, she gave a wave to her friends and seemed to glide along the sidewalk, still covered with chalk from break today.

"Hi, sweetie!" her mother yelled.

"Hi, mom!" Lori chanted. She swung the heavy door open and excitedly began to tell her mom all about her day at school as she plopped down in the passenger seat.

"I think Kevin Caudle is going to ask me to homecoming! And I got an A in on my trig test!"

Denise just smiled and congratulated her daughter on a job well done. When Lori slowed down, Denise began. "What do you think about yellow for the kitchen?"

She was smiling across at Lori and never saw the heavy dump truck careening down the hill from Wade Street.

"Mom! Watch out!" But Lori's scream came too late.

The dump truck plowed into the Buick doing sixty miles an hour. The initial bang was deafening as Denise lost consciousness. Lori felt a sudden and momentary feeling of weightlessness as her small frame was flung through the windshield and over the hood.

The brutal blow that the windshield inflicted gave way to a loud burst of noise, followed by complete silence. Lori never felt it, but as she hit the hard pavement of Wade Street, she slid twenty feet on her head, burning off most of her hair and cutting off her right ear.

The Buick's tires were still rolling, smoke billowing from somewhere underneath. The only other movement was Denise's arm as it gently landed on the backseat where her body had been shoved.

The dump truck continued to swerve uncontrollably until it finally hit an embankment, west of Greene Street. The driver, Deacon Mills, banged his head on the steering wheel as his limp body was tossed forward, then back. Blood poured from a gash in his forehead covering his eyes. He could hear voices, some yelling, while others were too muffled to understand.

Confused and hurt, he pushed the door open, stepped out of the truck, then collapsed on the hot pavement. He would live long enough for paramedics to arrive, but his punctured lung and broken ribs were too damaged.

As Deacon breathed his last breath, he could hear someone, somewhere, talking.

"Stay with us, man."

And then his world gave way to darkness.

Just a few yards away, another paramedic was fighting the urge to vomit at the sight lying at his feet. A young girl, maybe sixteen or seventeen, lay bloody, bald and severely disfigured. He knew she was dead, but could not resist the natural instinct to try and save her.

Her body lay still, helpless and vulnerable against the heat of the afternoon sun, so all he could do was cover her with his shirt. It wasn't much and was soaked with sweat, but it was all he could do for Lori Eades.

As he covered her, a neighbor, Lydia Kiker, was kneeling near the car, waiting for Denise to be pulled out of the wreckage. Lydia hoped with all her might that Denise was still alive, but as she looked into those gray eyes, blankly staring up at something she couldn't see, Lydia knew. She just knew that Denise was gone. Denise, Lori and Deacon were all gone.

Chapter One

1967
Six Years Earlier

Freddy Lee sat very still as he watched the people lining up outside of his front door. They all wore black or at least some combination of black.

Women fashioned small hats with tiny veils, men stuffed inside dark, hot suits. Most of them were crying, or had been crying, as was evident by eyes that were puffy and red.

Freddy was itchy inside his own black suit. He felt anxious as he heard his mother began to softly play the organ. It sounded so sad and final. She was playing *Precious Memories* as the crowd inched closer and closer to where he sat.

Hey, Fredlee! What 'ya thinking about, kid?

Freddy closed his eyes and tried desperately to drown out that annoying voice in his head. That voice that he assumed everyone heard. But this was *his* inside-voice that only he could hear. It had started back in August, just as school had resumed.

The kids in fourth grade always called Freddy *Fredlee*. He hated the way they did that. It was never Fred or Freddy, but *Fredlee,* as if Fred Lee was one name. They didn't call anyone else in school by their first and last name, just him.

Even his inside-voice called him Fredlee. Some days he could tune it out, but other days, like today, it was loud and piercing in his ear.

Come on, Fredlee. I know you can hear me. Why are you avoiding me?

Freddy squinted his eyes as he rose from the red velvet sofa. He never liked funeral home furniture. The dark mahogany tables and chair legs, the fabric on the seats. It was all so formal and final.

Freddy had a job to do today. Drowning out the voice, he walked across the floor and made his way to the door where the crowds were lined.

When his dad nodded his way, he opened the door and the mourners began to file in to the room. He shook hands with the men coming in and nodded at the ladies, the way his dad always had.

Fred Senior stood near the coffin, waiting to close its lid one final time. When Martha Dewberry began to wail loudly at the sight of her deceased husband, Fred stepped back and allowed her to kneel down near her husband's face. She softly kissed his lips and backed away.

Freddy felt sick as he watched that old woman kiss the dead man. That was disgusting to him. That man was cold, hard and had been dead for two days already. Why would she kiss that?

Lighten up, Fredlee. It ain't so bad kissing a corpse. I bet she'd slip him some tongue if his mouth weren't sewn shut.

Then the inside-voice began to make a repulsive sucking and slithering noise before bursting into a maniacal laugh.

Where did this come from? Freddy was terrified at the thoughts that flew through his mind. And throughout the service, he heard the same sounds over and over.

He couldn't make the voice or noises stop, no matter how hard he tried to block them out. His dad was going on and on about there being no more pain for Mr. Dewberry, no more death in heaven and how God Himself will wipe away our tears.

They were comforting and beautiful words to everyone else, but to Freddy, it was torture listening to them while trying to drown out the sounds coming from deep inside his head.

When the service was finally over, he helped his dad roll the coffin down the aisle of the chapel and into the back of the hearse. Fred Sr. walked back in and ushered Mrs. Dewberry to the family car. Freddy stood waiting to open the door for her.

Check that out, Fredlee. She lowered the whole damn car!

His inside voice was right, too. When she sat down, the car went about two inches lower and didn't bounce back. Mrs. Dewberry was a large old woman.

When she keels over, it'll take two coffins for her!

Freddy tried not to laugh at that notion. Even at ten years old, he knew better than to laugh out loud at a time like this. He shut the door as softly as he could and turned toward the hearse. He would ride along with his dad to Memorial Hall, the final resting place for the old man. Hampton Thomas, an associate from town, would drive the family car.

All the way to the mausoleum, Freddy thought about the family car following him. It was hard not to. His inside voice didn't' say anything else aside from fat jokes directed at Mrs. Dewberry.

Just think about that poor old man, Fredlee. Can you imagine a cow like that coming at you wanting to kiss you? I bet that man died from suffocation. I bet she lay down on top of him and he couldn't even breathe. She probably didn't even know he was dead until she rolled over and lit a cigarette!

Freddy wasn't amused. He really didn't even really know what sex was. How did his inside voice know so much? Dealing with that retched voice was making his head hurt worse than ever. It drained him completely when he had to ignore the sounds coming from within his small head.

By the time they arrived at Memorial, his brain was throbbing and Freddy was exhausted. He managed to help his dad pull the coffin out and when the pallbearers lined up, they allowed them to tote the old man to the building reserved for him.

Freddy was relieved to be done with this ordeal. When the final words were spoken and all the hands had been shook, he plopped down in the hearse and took in a deep breath.

He was sound asleep before they arrived back home. Thankfully Freddy's inside voice rested, too.

"Wake up, Freddy. We're home."

His dad nudged him gently until his little eyes cracked open. His mom was walking around the side of the house and smiled sweetly at her son as he climbed out.

Inside, the house was finally quiet again. Carolyn closed the parlor doors and took a deep breath.

"That was a lovely service, Fred. It really was."

Fred smiled as he took a seat at the kitchen table. He nodded in agreement as Carolyn sat down next to him. "I feel so sorry for Mrs. Dewberry. Such a sweet old lady. And they had been married for sixty-one years."

"He lived a long and prosperous life, dear. A long eighty year life and it was just his time," he said solemnly.

"Yes, I know. But it's still sad, you know? That poor woman will be so lost without him."

Fred knew she was right. Being a funeral director had taught him many things, but mostly that you never take the people you love for granted. They can easily be taken away in the blink of an eye. Fred himself had grown up in this house and his father had, too. Funerals and death were just a part of life for him. Carolyn had accepted that thirty years ago when she first met Fred. She had always supported him like a good and loving wife.

She had actually met him right here in this house. She was there to pay her respects to a relative who had passed. It wasn't a close family member and she wasn't upset, but she did notice the good-looking man standing at the foot of the coffin and offering his condolences to them all. And he had noticed her, too.

The next weekend, they went on their first date and five months later, they were married. It was love at first sight and had only grown stronger with time. Not long after marriage, Carolyn became pregnant with their first child, a baby girl. Tragically, even though doctors tried to tell her the baby was dead, she refused to believe. Carolyn went into labor at twenty-eight weeks and delivered her stillborn daughter. She named her Donna, after her mother, Donna Sue.

Fred prepared the small body for burial, but Carolyn was too weak to have a service. After she regained her strength, she went through several months of depression. Everything started to get back to normal eventually and they were so excited when they found out she was pregnant again. But that pregnancy was even shorter and the death of their second daughter, Emma seemed too much for Carolyn to bear.

Donna Sue and Fred decided that a state home for the mentally ill was in her best interest. Carolyn spent five months in that terrible home listening to incessant cries, moans and laughter.

When Fred brought her home, she seemed too distant, too down. It was five years before they would have their third child, a little boy, who lived for three whole days. Robert Benson Lee was buried beside his sisters, behind the family home.

Carolyn would lie over their graves until Fred would pull her in nightly. She was just too far-gone to ever try for another child. Her psychiatrist recommended sterilization, but when Carolyn begged and pleaded with Fred not to, he gave in and refused the surgery.

Six months later, she was carrying the one and only child that would live. There were two more babies that would be born, but Fred Lee Junior was the one son that would live. The five small markers that lined an area behind their home were kept clean and manicured.

Carolyn visited her children daily, but Freddy had made life worth living for her. Fred knew that if it weren't for Freddy, he wouldn't have a child *or* a wife.

Carolyn was a loving, tender woman that adored Freddy. She was so proud of him and did anything and everything she could to ensure he had a happy childhood.

The feelings she had and the voices she heard were still there, raging just below the surface. She vividly remembered the hospital, so she kept her thoughts and feelings to herself. She would never go back there. Carolyn never told another soul about the voices she heard. And she would never know that her son heard them, too.

Chapter Two

Carolyn and Fred were asleep. Freddy tossed and turned from side to side. He tried everything to get still, but sleep would not come for Freddy that night. Eventually, he got up and made his way down to the family room and squatted down in front of the television.

The old black and white set was all snow at first, but with a little adjusting, a clear picture formed in front of him. He turned the dial until he found *The Little Rascals* and settled down on the vinyl-covered couch.

He wrestled with a blanket and when he had finally snuggled in just right, he opened a box of Little Mints cookies and tried to relax. So far, his inside-voice had been pleasantly quiet.

He still couldn't get past the thoughts he'd had. He was still seeing an image of the heavy Mrs. Dewberry waddling closer and closer to that casket and bending down to kiss her late husband. In his mind, he saw her looking up at him and smiling just before her tongue slipped into the corpse's mouth.

As he reminisced over the images, he spit his cookie out in to his hand and jumped up to run to the sink. The kitchen was just through the doorway. The house was designed with an open floor plan, very unusual for an older construction like this one. Each room circled around, giving the feeling of a round house.

When he was much smaller, Freddy loved riding his tricycle around and around, going from one room to the other. The only rooms he shied away from were the front rooms of the home.

Inside the living room was a door that led into the parlor. This part of the house had square rooms. The walls were a dark pine and the floors creaked under each footstep. The red velvet upholstery and the dark wood accents coupled with the creaky floorboards gave the whole parlor an eerie feel.

Freddy never came in here unless he was expected to help with services or arrangements. At ten years old, there wasn't a big need for him just yet. When he did have to go in, he hurried to do what had to be done and left as quickly as possible. He could always feel someone—or some*thing*—watching him and he hated that feeling.

The air itself was different there. He hated the pink lighting, too. It was supposed to give the corpse a more natural glow, but to his young mind, it just seemed odd. Pink lights and red furnishings were just creepy.

As he made his way back into the living room, the TV had gone to snow again. He was starting to feel more relaxed, so he flipped the dial to off and settled under his blanket and closed his eyes.

That was the morning he had his first real nightmare—the Saturday that his dreams seemed to become a reality.

To start with, the room was just dark. But soon, a thick fog began to fill in around him. He could hear someone calling his name, but he couldn't see who it was. He could hear people talking and some crying.

As he walked ahead, he realized he was inches from the parlor and that those rooms were full of people. He was no longer walking now, but gliding. Gliding against his will closer and closer to an open coffin. At first, it seemed empty. But suddenly he saw that there was someone inside.

It was him. His small body lay in the coffin, dressed in his little black suit. His hands were folded over each other, as he had seen so many times before.

His heart began racing and he could hear it roaring inside his ears. He didn't want to look, but he couldn't seem to stop himself, either. As his body came to a stop, the Freddy in the coffin opened his eyes and began to speak. At first, it was very quiet, but became louder and louder as he continued to talk.

Listen up, Fredlee. Soon, you'll be dead. You'll be dead and I'll take over. I'm going to rock this joint! I'm going to make everyone see that you were never worth living to start with. They'll love me the most and you'll soon be completely forgotten. Got that? You'll be dead and gone and I'll be the Freddy everyone loves. You ain't worth shit, you little prick. You're a nothing. A loser. No one even likes you, well, except for mommy dearest. But soon enough, she'll be gone, too. I'll make sure of that.

Freddy couldn't breathe. He couldn't move. He could hear people talking all around him, but he was frozen in place with fear.

As the fog lifted, he could see the room was actually empty. There was no one here. Where did they go? He was finally able to draw a breath in and turned to face the creepy room. He took in every corner of the darkness and the morbid walls right down to the heavy brown drapes that hung still and stale over the picture windows.

He was yelling now. Screaming, really.

"Stop it! I'm not dead! I'm right here! I'm not dead and you're not real! Shut up! Just shut up and go away!"

He could hear his inside-voice laughing. It sounded much huskier and scratchier than his, but it was fading away as his eyes opened to see the sun had risen and the living room was no longer dark. He was relieved to know that it was just a dream. He was soaked with sweat under the blanket, but he was alive and well.

"It was just a dream," he whispered.

Chapter Three

1971
Four Years Later

Freddy sat in his room after school, listening to records. He heard the phone ring, but didn't bother to get up. Carolyn was home and she would no doubt answer. Five minutes later, Carolyn knocked on Freddy's door.

"Freddy? May I come in?"

"Sure, mom!" Freddy yelled over his music. He turned the volume down as his mom walked in. She sat down on the edge of his bed and smiled at him.

"Something wrong, mom?"

"Well, I have something to tell you, Freddy."

Freddy took a deep breath. This was never a good thing.

"Okay, what's up?"

"Miss Kate Becker passed away."

Freddy wasn't too surprised by that. Miss Kate had cancer and had been sick a long time. She had taken a leave of absence from school where she taught ninth grade English. Freddy never got to have her. By the time he'd entered ninth grade, she was too sick to teach. He had seen her, though. She was a beautiful woman with long, dark hair. She actually looked more like a student, a senior maybe, but a student either way.

She always wore short skirts and the boys loved it. They always turned to look when she walked down the halls. The girls liked her, too. She was young and lively and fun to be around. She seemed to skip when she walked. Most of the students didn't realize just how young she was. She had only been teaching for two years when she was diagnosed with cancer. And now, at only twenty-six, she was dead.

"Oh, I'm sorry to hear that. She was a sweet lady," Freddy commented.

There really wasn't a lot to say. They all knew she was dying. She was already too sick for treatments when the doctor found the cancer. She had been bed ridden for several months and in a small town, word travels fast. They'd heard that any day, she'd die.

"Yes, I am too. I know things will be tough at school tomorrow and if you want to stay home, I'll write you an excuse. I don't want you getting so upset."

"Oh, I'm fine, mom. Really. I never had Miss Kate and didn't really know her. I'll be fine to go."

Carolyn patted his knee and sat staring at him for a while longer. The glare made Freddy feel very uncomfortable.

"Mom? You okay?"

Carolyn blinked and smiled. "Yes, dear. I'm fine. I just wanted you to know before you got to school tomorrow and found out. Oh, and one more thing. The family has requested our services, so after school tomorrow, you may need to help your dad."

For several months now, Fred had been considering letting Freddy help more with the family business. Freddy really wanted to. In fact, he knew that eventually he'd be running the funeral parlor. He'd never really considered doing anything else. Other kids dreamed of fighting in Vietnam or going to college for teaching degrees or to become doctors and lawyers. But until eighth grade career day, he never really considered any other future. And this still seemed better than fighting a war.

If college were anything like high school, then he'd rather not go. The kids were always teasing Freddy. He assumed it was because he was a gawky, tall teen with feet longer than his body and acne. Maybe it was because his family owned the funeral home. Sometimes, he'd hear them humming *The Adams Family* theme song when they saw him coming.

They had truly made his school days miserable. But his mom assured him that they would grow up and mature and he would be fine. He wanted to believe her, but he couldn't help hating most of the kids there. They hated him right back.

Freddy was thrilled at the possibility of getting to help his dad. It would at least give him something to do after school and maybe it would make college a little easier. He nodded and smiled as Carolyn stood and walked away. She closed his door behind her and left him to his music.

Downstairs, Fred was waiting for her. When Carolyn entered the kitchen, he looked to her and winked.

"It's a shame. Kate was a sweet girl and so young."

Carolyn agreed. "It might help to know that Freddy is interested in helping you tomorrow."

Fred smiled and shook his head. "Well, I guess I'll head on over there and collect the body."

"Fred, that sounds so cold."

"Okay. I'm going to get Miss Kate now and I'll be home soon."

Carolyn giggled and hugged her husband goodbye.

Freddy heard the wagon crank up and walked over to his window. He watched his dad back down the driveway. He knew he was going to get Miss Kate.

Won't be long now, Fredlee. That smokin' hot chick will be here soon. I can't wait! Are you as excited as I am?

Freddy tried to drown the voice out by turning up the volume on his stereo, but he couldn't.

That's okay, Fredlee. I know you hear me. You don't have to answer. I know you hear me loud and clear.

And then it laughed again.

Freddy knew it was right, though. Miss Kate was, well, had been, smoking hot. She was beautiful in every sense of the word. And he was soon to see her again.

* * * * * * * *

The next day, after a very uneventful day of school, Freddy hurried home to help his dad. There had been plenty of kids crying and some that left early. He knew he was supposed to feel something, but all he felt was anxiety as he waited to get back home. There was no need for him to feel anything. He barely knew Miss Kate. He only saw her a few times before she'd had to quit teaching.

This was the first *real* corpse he'd ever seen. He headed up the drive way and turned left towards the building out to the side. This area wasn't a part of the house, but a separate workspace entirely. Fred was already working when Freddy entered the small building.

"Hey, champ!" Fred spoke when he saw his son.

"Hi. What are you doing?"

"Well, I'll tell you exactly what I'm doing as I work. You just watch this time and eventually, you'll be doing a lot to help out."

Freddy nodded and perched himself up on a stool near his father.

"Our job is to make a client look his or her best before family and friends come to pay their respects. A corpse isn't peaceful looking until we make it that way. In order to get there, we prepare the body. I prefer the term client, but to each his own."

Freddy was mesmerized by the equipment, tools and supplies that surrounded him. It was his first time inside this work area.

"A body brought to us more than likely still has food, water and other things in it. We have to clean it out. When we get it all clean inside, we replace all that with something else. This process is what we call embalming."

Freddy knew a few things already. After all, he was a teenager and he had watched *Frankenstein, The Bride of Frankenstein* and *The Mummy.* He'd read all about how Egyptians had prepared their recently departed and made mummies. He just nodded as his dad continued.

"It's much easier to do a few other things first."

When Fred pulled the body from the metal drawer near the back of the room, a white, clean sheet covered it. But there were spots on the sheet here and there.

"That's just a little liquid, Freddy. We'll take care of all that, too".

When he pulled the sheet back, Freddy saw a beautiful woman, too young to be here. Her hair was still long and flowing. Freddy always thought that when a person had cancer, their hair fell out, but Fred explained that chemotherapy caused the hair loss, not the disease.

"Why didn't she have treatments, dad? She could still be alive."

"Well, son, not everyone can tolerate the same things. Miss Kate was very sick when her doctor found the cancer. Her body wasn't strong enough by then. It just wouldn't have worked."

He watched as Fred washed her carefully, then brushed and styled her hair the best he could. He slid a small piece of cotton underneath her eyelids, and then neatly glued them shut. All the while, he talked to Freddy, explaining what and why he was doing each thing. After he'd stuffed cotton in her mouth to fill in the sunken places, he wired her jaw shut. Next, he added a light dusting of a powder makeup, giving Miss Kate a pretty, lifelike complexion again. The pink he sprinkled on her cheeks gave her a healthy, summer glow.

Freddy felt his stomach twisting into a tight pretzel as Fred inserted a needle into her abdomen.

"Some embalmers choose the neck, while others find a main vein in the arm. I do it this way so there won't be any visible marks to hide before visitation and it works just as good. And I've found that it's faster, too."

He turned on a big, yellow tank and watched in disgust as Miss Kate's bodily fluids rushed out into a bucket placed on the floor. The smell was gut-wrenching. It smelled like a cross between medicine and vomit with a little touch of diarrhea added to the aromatic blend.

How could anyone so pretty stink so horribly? Freddy wanted to ask. But he knew his dad wouldn't appreciate him talking about Miss Kate that way.

Two hours later, when the last of the bile spewed out, Fred turned off the machine. He swapped out tubes and equipment, and then turned it on again. This one sounded like an old car, humming and spitting and shaking the floor around him.

"And that's that, son. That's about all there is to it. Not too bad, is it?"

Freddy wanted to scream and run away and puke his own contents out. He wished he could tell his dad just how terrible this whole system was. But instead, he shook his head and smiled.

"Nope. Not bad at all. So, what's next?"

"Well, when the machine is all done, we'll dress her and place her in a coffin. The family picked the one they want and I ordered it this morning. Hampton Thomas will deliver it tomorrow, more than likely. It's going to be awhile before this is all done, so if you want to go back to the house, you can."

Freddy didn't have to be told twice. He ran from the building as fast as he could. When he'd run himself out, he was in his room. He didn't even remember climbing the stairs or going in. But here he was. And for days, all he could smell was that terrible stench oozing out of Miss Kate. Every time he closed his eyes, he saw her lying there, helpless and empty. When the family arrived two nights later to view their loved one, they all talked about how pretty she was and how natural she looked and that it looked like she was just asleep.

He'd heard all of that before. But he knew Miss Kate wasn't sleeping and he knew that if they could have seen her lying on that work table getting her piss pushed out and her eyes glued shut, they wouldn't think she was so pretty.

For the past two days, he'd heard his inside voice louder than ever.

Look at that hot chick, will ya, Fredlee? Wouldn't you love to crack open that cold one and enjoy the feel of her wrapped around you? You know you would. You don't have to lie to me, Fredlee. I see it, too. Man, that lady is smoking hot! What do ya say, Fredlee? When the crowd dies down and the folks are asleep, let's you and me go visit with the old lady. Let Miss Kate turn you into a man!

And the inside-voice laughed wildly in his ear. It was gross, thinking like that. It wasn't right. Why would he think those things? What was wrong with him?

Freddy pulled a pillow down over his head and tried desperately to drown out the incessant voice. He cradled his knees and rocked back and forth, begging it to stop, to shut up. He didn't know what made his inside-voice say these things. He tried to keep it quiet. He found that the only way to do that was to make it happy. If he did what the inside-voice said, it would leave him alone—for a while, anyway.

On the night of November 3, 1971, he made his inside-voice very happy and proud. Other boys his age were stretching their pathetic necks to look up girls' skirts. They were whispering in the boys' room about seeing cleavage and wondering what sex was all about. Freddy would smile to himself and pretend not to listen. He already knew what it was all about. His inside-voice had helped him see that he could have any woman he desired, as long as she was in his daddy's building, cold and stiff and wanting him like he wanted her.

That night, he lay in the coffin with Miss Kate. He slowly touched her arm, feeling the coldness throughout his hand. Softly, he allowed his hand to caress her cheeks, her hair and her neck. Once he grew accustomed to the stiffness of her limbs, he relaxed and felt himself becoming more and more aroused. His hands awkwardly grabbed at her breasts and as he found his way up her pretty, short skirt, he knew he could do this.

He climbed on top of her and as he penetrated her cold, hard flesh, he heard Miss Kate moan. He felt her nails clawing down his back. He pulled her legs up around him and she squeezed him tightly as they both climaxed together.

He heard her voice telling him how much she appreciated what he'd done. She'd needed it for so long, he thought her heard her say. He pulled her arm over his chest and manipulated her hand to stroke the handful of hair that had sprouted here and there.

When he'd climbed out and repositioned her just right, he closed the coffin and skipped back up to his room. His inside-voice never spoke, but it didn't have to. It was proud of Freddy. For the first time in a long time, Freddy slept soundly with no nightmares at all.

As Freddy got ready for the graveside service the next day, he stood looking at himself in the mirror. He was still just an awkward teenage boy. He was taller than most of the kids his age and his dark hair was becoming a deep shade of black. For some reason, puberty had brought on the change of color in his hair, his acne and a very strong inside-voice.

Chapter Four

September 25, 1973
The Day Lori Eades Died

Freddy sat perched on a big rock behind his house. Even though the sun had almost completely set, it was still too hot. He wiped away the perspiration from his eyes with his forearm. He knew what had happened. He heard his father talking hours ago and knew all about Lori and her mother. He also knew about the truck driver, Deacon. Deacon wasn't local. No one even knew for sure who he was. But everyone knew Lori.

Lori Eades was a very pretty girl—the kind of girl that made Freddy nervous. She had long, blonde hair that was normally gathered in a straight ponytail, up high. She had all these bows that matched her clothes and every day she wore one. Freddy tried to remember. *What color did she wear today? Wasn't it red?* For the life of him, he couldn't recall. He tried not to look at her too long. If he did, it was likely some boy would notice and start with the teasing again.

His mind was jolted back to the present as the sound of a motor slowly drove in and around the building that stood thirty or so yards from the house. Freddy felt butterflies swimming around in his stomach. The car pulling up in his yard held the body of either Denise or Lori Eades. He heard the back door open and saw his dad walking across the white pebbles that formed the neat driveway leading to the building and the house.

The white driveway wasn't very long, but as it grew closer to the house, it branched off and led to either the building or the front yard. This car would circle around the building, stopping at the far side.

Fred walked casually along the drive toward his son. Freddy heard the crunching of the pebbles under his dad's feet. When Fred was close enough to Freddy, he placed a warm hand on his shoulder.

"You shouldn't help this time, son. Go inside and help your mother set the table. I'll be in soon."

"But, dad, I want to help. I'm fine. This is, well, the last thing I can do to help a classmate, a friend."

Fred smiled, pleased with his son. For a teenager, Freddy was very mature and professional. Fred had no doubt that someday his son would take over and continue the family business.

"You know, I think it's about time to change that sign out front."

"You mean it, dad?"

Freddy felt a lump in his throat as he and his dad both turned to face the sign. The sign he was referring to was the *Lee Funeral Parlor and Chapel* sign that swung from a white fence post at the end of the drive. Fred laughed a small bit as he forgot momentarily what awaited him.

"Lee and Son Funeral Parlor and Chapel has a nice ring to it, don't you think?"

"Yes, sir. It sure does."

It wasn't until they heard a familiar voice from the building that brought them back to the work at hand.

"Well, are you sure? I could use the help, with three bodies and all."

"I'm up for it, dad. I promise," Freddy chimed.

And so the two walked together, father's' arm around son as they made their way into what was sure to be a long night.

Mr. Knight, the EMS driver, nodded at Fred as he walked around to the back of the station wagon and opened the swinging door. Inside, he could see one body on a gurney, strapped in place and covered with a tarp.

"I'll head back for the girl when we unload."

Fred nodded and carefully pulled the gurney toward him.

Freddy stepped inside the building, switched on the light and waited for the room to brighten. The electricity hummed briefly. The bulbs blinked a few times and then were on full force. He had done this before and knew what to do.

He clutched the stretcher with both hands. The metal frame felt cool against his clammy skin. He began to back out of the room, towing the stretcher behind him. As he pulled the table along the sidewalk that led to the far side of the building, he couldn't help but feel anxious. He had helped his dad do this many times already, but never for someone his age and never for someone this pretty.

It's all I can do now for a classmate, a friend, he'd said.

Freddy smiled to himself as he rolled those words around in his head. He could never tell his dad that Lori wasn't a friend. She hated him, he guessed. Most of the kids in the town did. But he wanted to do this. It seemed to him, it was the last thing he could do to get even with someone that constantly ignored him.

This was his chance to finally get even with someone that laughed at him the day he wet his pants in third grade. His chance to get even with someone that made fun of him when he tripped in the hallway last week, spilling books and pencils and paper all over the place. His chance at revenge. He was going to embalm Lori Eades.

Fred gently rolled Denise Eades from the gurney in back of the wagon to the stretcher Freddy had retrieved. Giving the gurney a firm push, it slid back in to the car with a long, dull squeak. Any other time, Mr. Knight might have commented about the squeaky wheels and the dry grid beneath it, but now was not the time.

"Be back in thirty minutes, maybe an hour," he softly said to Fred.

"I'll be here," Fred retorted.

Then together he and his son rolled the body of Denise Eades inside the building. This was the workstation, as Fred called it.

There wasn't anything too badly damaged on Denise.

"Internal damage," Fred said.

The building gave his voice an eerie echo. The summer heat and stillness didn't help. The effect made his voice sound like it had come from a two hundred fifty pound body builder, when, in fact, he was more like one hundred fifty pounds. The sound made Freddy jump a little regardless. He was glad his dad didn't notice. He might send him back inside regardless of what Freddy thought or wanted.

But Fred was concentrating too now to notice anything. Thirty minutes later, the sound of the wagon pulling up the drive made Freddy stand.

"I'll go meet Mr. Knight, dad," Freddy whispered.

He had thought that his own voice might pull Fred out of this work-induced trance and change his mind on letting him help. Very gently, he helped his dad roll Denise onto a stainless steel table to await preparations. Then Freddy wheeled the stretcher back out to the far side of the building all by himself to greet Mr. Knight and Lori.

Don't get your hopes up, kid. This could be the fat greasy truck driver with the gash in his head and the ribs sticking out of his beer gut. Don't go getting too excited. Stay calm, Fredlee.

Mr. Knight nodded again for the second time. Freddy nodded back and continued to roll the stainless steel stretcher toward him smoothly and calmly, just in case it was Lori.

"Meet Mr. Deacon Mills," Mr. Knight said.

Freddy could feel his face deflate at the words. He was getting more and more nervous as he waited. As he walked around to the back of the wagon, his foot got in his way and he tripped over the root of an old elm.

Oh, that's just frickin great, Fredlee. Show 'em just how smooth you are, will 'ya? Get us kicked right out of here, will 'ya? You're a real joke, you know that?

Freddy's inside-voice was yelling loudly in his ears.

"Steady there, Fredlee," Mr. Knight shouted.

Freddy could feel his face growing red with embarrassment and with anger. Even the grownups around here knew him as Fredlee. Then he remembered that Mr. Knight had a twelve-year-old daughter, Robin. Undoubtedly, even the younger kids called him that, too.

Freddy grabbed the clipboard from Mr. Knight and quickly signed the paperwork. Handing it back to him, Freddy turned the stretcher and began walking away. Over his shoulder, he heard the old fat man laughing to himself.

Why don't you take that pen from 'em and shove up clear up his nose, Fredlee? That'll show him! Do it, Fredlee! Do it!

Freddy ignored the inside-voice and entered the building with Deacon Mills. His meaty body jiggled around at the bumps in the doorway and that made Freddy's inside-voice laugh again. Freddy was growing exhausted. Tuning the voice out was tiring and stressful.

Freddy turned back to see Mr. Knight pushing himself into the station wagon. When he settled into the driver's seat, the car went down a few inches. He slammed the door, making Freddy jump again. His inside-voice was saying all sorts of things now. He grabbed the stretcher with both hands to steady himself and rolled on until he was completely inside with his dad.

Fred had put on an opera eight-track and it filled the space with melody. He'd rather the music was anything else, but this was his dad's work music, so he didn't complain. He rolled the table along until he had reached a long, wide wall of stainless steel drawers. There were five drawers in all, but they had never had them all filled at once.

Freddy had heard about the Spanish Flu of 1918 and how so many bodies were stacked together, no room for them all. He had heard about an apartment fire ten years ago when the remains of eighteen people were carried to several different morgues for storage. But he'd never seen more than two bodies here at the time. Now, it would house three of them.

Freddy pushed down on the drawer lever and heard it unseal. Pulling it open, he could feel the cold air hit his face in a rush. He pulled the tarp from Deacon Mills, revealing two ribs that protruded from his midsection, a cut just above his brow bone and several pricks here and there that told of glass from a windshield or a side mirror. It would be his job to remove the glass splinters and clean, glue and conceal the gash on his head. The ribs wouldn't be so hard. They could simply be cut in two and discarded. A clean shirt and suit jacket and voila! No one would ever know the difference. And from the looks of it, Mr. Deacon Mills wasn't going to tell anyone, either.

Freddy slid Deacon's body into the freezer drawer, where he would have to wait his turn. When the tray could move no farther in, Freddy pushed the stretcher to his right and locked the latch on the drawer. As he made his way to the far end of the building, he heard his dad humming along to the operatic drama spilling out into the dense air. He made his way to the far side of the building and reached for a new tray to line the stretcher.

When he had done all he could do, he stood and watched his dad working on Mrs. Eades. He had already sprayed her body down, removing most of the glass fragments and all of the blood. Even though she was already pale and seemingly bloodless, there was much left to do.

Fred worked diligently to do what had to be done. The embalming process would actually come last, as he had found over the years that the inner work was easier handled last.

Not too much later, headlights bounced on the opposite wall and Freddy knew what that meant. Lori had finally arrived.

Fred looked up momentarily as Freddy chimed in. "I'll take care of it, dad."

He grabbed the paperwork he knew Mr. Knight would require and took hold of the stretcher. As he began rolling it down the incline, Freddy saw that the wagon had already come to a stop.

Mr. Knight climbed out, letting out a grunt as he stood. He wobbled around to the back of the wagon one last time. Freddy looked on in anticipation as Lori was slid out of place. The bag that contained her was thick and black. Freddy hated it at once. But he kept his mouth shut and signed the papers.

Normally, Mr. Knight would require an adult signature, but at this moment, the man on the moon could have signed them. He was too tired to care. It had been an awful day. He hadn't worked an all day job like this in ten years. And the night of the apartment fire, it had been cold and snowy. Not the gosh awful heat he was working in now. He just wanted to go home, shower and wash this day away.

"Thank you, Mr. Knight. And don't you worry. I'll take good care of Robin for you."

"What's that, Fredlee?"

"I'll take good care of Lori."

Mr. Knight gave a half grin, half frown as he watched Freddy pushing Lori up toward the building. He could have sworn that oddity called Lori by his daughter's name. He shrugged his shoulders as he cranked up to leave. He was obviously exhausted and couldn't leave this place fast enough.

Chapter Five

As Freddy entered the building, Fred was just finishing up on Denise.

"Ah, right on time!" he commended his son.

Freddy eased the stretcher up to the steel table and stopped.

"Let's take care of Lori before we get to Mr. Deacon okay, dad? I just feel, I don't know, like the girls should always come first."

Fred gave little thought to Freddy's suggestion and shrugged his shoulders. He didn't care which body came next. They were all the same as far as he was concerned. The process would be the same no matter which came first, next or last.

Fred covered Denise, a pale and lifeless vessel still starring up at the ceiling. The rest of the preparations could wait. As he pushed Denise from the table to a stretcher, Freddy began to unzip the bag, which held Lori. He didn't know how his dad could stuff Denise in to that drawer as quickly as he did, but seconds later, he was standing right next to Freddy, patiently waiting.

Freddy was savoring the moment. He wanted to see, but he didn't want to see. He was excited, but full of dread. He was more confused than ever when his inside-voice piped up.

"Jerk the zipper, Fredlee. Come on, we don't have all night. Get the lead out!"

Slowly, the zipper began to make a high-pitched noise as Freddy's fingers tugged at it. Just as the bag began to pull apart, the opera rose to an even higher pitch. It was like the moment was made just for him. Like he was part of a movie with perfect background music working the audience into a frenzy.

And just as the highest soprano finished her solo, the room became deafeningly quiet, except for the slow tug of that darned zipper that seemed to be stuck on something.

"Here, let me help you," Fred recommended.

And sure enough, the zipper was stuck on something. A little harder tug revealed not only a very badly disfigured Lori, but also a piece of meat about the size of a dime clinging to the inside teeth of the zipper.

"Sometimes, when it's really bad like this, when the body has been mangled up, that happens. But not to worry. We're going to pretty her up, right, son?"

Freddy was fighting the urge to puke all over Lori, but managed a nod. He couldn't take his eyes off of her.

Just this morning, she wore a red skirt that revealed legs that had been freshly shaven. Her red bow was the exact shade of that mini skirt. And now, she was nothing more than road kill.

Fred was too concentrated on his tasks to notice Freddy heaving, but as soon as the first sound emitted from his mouth, he quickly turned away from Lori.

He didn't want her to see him throwing up.

How could he let her see that? She would think he was a dork all over again. Like when he fell last week or when he tripped over Henry Dooley's size twelve's in geography on the second day of the school year.

Truth be known, Henry Dooley placed his large foot right in Freddy's path. He was hoping the dork would trip, but when he fell and slid three feet across the floor, it was more than Henry could have imagined. It was a riot that earned Henry a high-five from Jack Wincill and a smile from Lori Eades. And even though Mrs. Fletcher reprimanded Henry, she too had snickered at Freddy. So how could he let Lori see him puke now? He couldn't.

Embarrassed, he ran from the building and into the house. The screen door slammed behind him as he ran up the stairs, kicked his door closed, and collapsed on his bed.

Seriously? You're going to cry? Give me a frickin' break, Fredlee. Grow a pair, already! This is the one time you can get your revenge. Everyone will know that you had a hand in Lori's final destination. Everyone will know that you are a force to be reckoned with. Now, get back out there and show Fred Lee Senior just how ballsy his son is. Get up, you coward! Get up and do this!

Freddy wiped away a stream of fresh sweat. Maybe it was exhaustion, maybe it was cowardice or maybe it was just a sixteen year old being a sixteen year old, but he had to do this. He had to watch as the last drop of blood drained from Lori Eades cold, dead body.

As he walked back into the building, Fred stood there watching him. He had removed Lori from the bag and placed her on the table and covered her with a clean, fresh sheet, but that was all.

"Can you do this, son? You don't have to, you know."

"Yeah, I know. But I owe it to Lori."

With that, Fred turned on the water and Freddy watched as the showerhead began to slowly rinse away the trauma of a fatal wreck.

Fred looked up and saw that it was ten o'clock.

"This is a good place to stop, anyway. It's late and tomorrow is a school day. We'll resume our work as soon as you get home from school, okay? You go get washed up and hit the hay. I'm sure you're tired and to tell you the truth, I am too."

Freddy nodded and tiredly walked back across the yard to their home. He never used the front door. The front doors led into the parlor and he avoided those rooms no matter how tired he was.

Sometimes, if the corpse was an elderly person, or even a younger one that hadn't suffered, the mood might not be so sad. But in cases like the ones coming, there was never a happy moment, laughter in the background or even a smile. And this was the part of the funeral home business Freddy hated. The atmosphere in those rooms was too thick and sad even for him.

As he walked around the house to the kitchen entrance, he was too tired to think about Lori. He was too tired to shower or even eat. He made his way upstairs and collapsed on his bed.

He had no way of knowing that the inside-voice he felt was more than just a voice. He had a whole other being in him just waiting to escape. Fighting that voice and trying to keep the other Freddy in was almost too much. He was asleep before his head ever hit the pillow.

Freddy was sound asleep when Lori entered his dream. She walked slowly across the floor to his bed and stood staring down at him. Gradually she bent over him, smiling. He could see the red bow in her hair and smell the faint scent of Puppy Love perfume.

Presently, Freddy smiled back and realized he must be dreaming. Lori Eades would never smile at him or even get close enough for him to recognize her fragrance.

"Don't worry, Fredlee. I'm watching you. I know what you want to do to me. I'm watching."

And then, almost instantly, Freddy was awake. He lay there sweating profusely as he tried to catch his breath in the thick air of his room. Realizing it was just a dream, Freddy rolled on to his side, trying to fall back into a new dream. But seconds turned to minutes and minutes turned to hours. After two hours of tossing back and forth, he sat up on the edge of his bed and swiped away the perspiration.

Freddy just could not get Lori out of his brain. He stood, pulled on a pair of shorts and made his way into the hallway. He could only hear the sound of the old grandfather clock at the end of the hall going tick tock, tick tock through the warm September night. As he stood listening, he was jolted by the clock's dong.

*Dong...dong...dong...*and then it stopped.

Three am, Freddy thought.

Then his inside-voice started again.

Go look at Lori, Fredlee. Go check her out. And by the way, she ain't watchin' you. She ain't watchin' nothin'. Trust me. She's dead and gone, Fredlee. That thing in the building out back? Just a shell. An empty shell and nothing more. You could light firecrackers up her ass. She ain't wakin' up.

Freddy stopped by his parents' room and listened. He could hear the little tufts made by his mom. He could hear his dad snoring away. They were sound asleep, so Fred made his way to the building behind the house.

He just couldn't get the thought out of his mind. All he could picture was that beautiful girl, red bow and soft, sweet smell. He carefully and quietly opened the building, placing the keys in the pocket of his shorts.

Just one quick look. That's all. Just one quick look and I'm outta here, he thought to himself.

His inside-voice was surprisingly quiet now. That was a huge relief for Freddy. He heard it most all of the time now, sometimes even while he slept. It was so hard to focus on anything else with that voice screaming in his brain.

Freddy couldn't believe how still, how quiet the morgue seemed without his dad there with *Madame Butterfly* yelping away. Freddy tiptoed to the heavy, metal drawer. He knew exactly where Lori was resting.

He pulled on the door and the drawer opened effortlessly. He began to slide Lori out of her cocoon and noticed that his dad had covered her with the sheet again. When Lori was all the way out, he stood momentarily, wondering if maybe he should just push her back in and let her be.

No, he needed to look at her. Other kids were going to see her in two, possibly three days. Her father and brothers would be there, too. Crying, wailing, all pathetic. No one should cry over her. There was no one at Bowman High that deserved crying and wailing and mourning, no matter how they'd died.

Freddy had wondered many times why he didn't feel the same emotions as other people. While they were upset and emotional wrecks, he simply looked on at them in awe. He never cried. He never felt sorry for people. He just felt empty inside. His inside-voice was the only thing that seemed to keep him sane, and yet when it spoke, he wanted to scream.

Then, as he thought about how mean Lori had been, he jerked the sheet back. There she lay, all clean and pale. Without the blood and ooze, she really didn't even look half bad.

Well, there *was* the loss of that ear and the baldness. But he knew once his dad finished, she would look almost as good as new.

He reached down and gently stroked her lifeless cheek. Yes, she had been mean to him, but now, as she lay there helpless, he realized that maybe he'd never really given Lori the chance to change her mind about him. Maybe with age, she would have grown to like him.

Chapter Six

The next day at school was somber. Everyone was saddened, even the teachers.

"May I have your attention students, teachers and faculty," the voice began over the intercom. Mr. Richardson, the principal, was as heartbroken as anyone.

"In light of yesterday's terrible tragedy, all sporting activities are hereby canceled until further notice. Also, the Eades family is planning visitation and will let us know when services will be held. Teachers, please be considerate of your students today as they try to comprehend this tragic loss. Now, if you will, please join me in a moment of silence as we remember Lori Eades."

After that long and painful moment, the teacher, Mrs. Long, blew her nose, wiped away some really dark stained tears and sat down behind her desk. All the kids looked at her for a long while until finally she spoke.

"I know how lovable Lori was and how much you'll miss her. It's hard to know just what to say, but we should remember that Lori is with Jesus and her mother. She is not alone and she is in no pain."

Tears began to fill her eyes again and she waited a few minutes before resuming. "Does anyone need to see a guidance counselor?"

Mrs. Long waited as two girls got up and went to her desk. Lori's friend, Veronica, said she needed help. They had drawn the school mascot, a Bearcat, on the sidewalk just yesterday in preparation for homecoming.

The other girl, Pamela, only nodded. Mrs. Long stood quietly and led them out into the hallway. The other students couldn't make out the words, but they didn't have to. Mrs. Long was pointing and giving them directions to the nurse's station. There they would be seen by a psychiatrist, Dr. Millard, a local doctor that had come in voluntarily to offer assistance and counseling.

As Mrs. Long took her seat again, she asked, "Did anyone do their reading assignment last night?"

One boy, a tall thin boy with dark hair raised his hand. Freddy was the only one that had actually done his work. He was also the only one that didn't seem affected by Lori's death. Some of the students snickered under their breaths, but Mrs. Long only smiled at him.

"Thank you, Freddy. How about you start us on the next chapter?"

Freddy nodded, opened his book and began to read aloud from *Billy Bud.* As he began, other students slowly began to open their books, too. Mrs. Long wanted to go home and cry her eyes out, but she knew that this was for the best—to try and carry on and remain as normal as possible. Just make it through the day.

The rest of the day dragged on, as every teacher and ever student did and said the same things over and over. How they just couldn't believe it, how they were so shocked and how they didn't know what poor old Roger Eades would do without his wife and daughter.

Three o'clock finally came and Freddy headed home. The walk from school wasn't that far. His home was only four blocks away. As he walked along, he couldn't help thinking about what the day would hold. His dad was waiting for him. Well, he had promised, anyway. And even though Lori had been washed down and cleaned, there were other things to do.

When he finally made his way in through the kitchen door, his mother was baking brownies.

"Hi there, champ!" Carolyn Lee sang out. "How was your day? Was it as bad as I'm thinking?"

"No, not too bad. The kids were sad, but we got through it."

Carolyn nodded as she placed a warm brownie on the table in front of him. She loved her son and wanted more children so badly. After so many heartbreaks and the loss of other babies, she had resolved to be the best mother to Freddy that she could be. He was a very special child and she strove to make him feel it.

Carolyn stared at her son, lost in thought. She got lost in thought quite a lot. It always made Freddy feel so uncomfortable when she stared at him. Actually, she stared through him, as if he was no longer there.

"Where's dad?"

Freddy waited and when Carolyn didn't seem to hear him, he asked again.

"Mom, where is dad?"

He patted her hand and that brought her back to the present, as it had many times before. "Where is dad?" Freddy softly spoke.

"Oh, I'm sorry, Freddy. I guess I was in my own world again, huh?"

"Yeah, I guess."

Freddy's voice drifted off as Carolyn stood and walked toward the kitchen windows.

"Your dad said to tell you to come out to the building as soon as you could. But Freddy, I'm worried that this is too much for you, working on someone so young. I know that Lori was your friend. I'm just afraid it's too much for you."

Carolyn didn't know about the hard times her son faced at school. As far as she knew, he was as happy and normal as any other teenager. But this tragedy was hard for the adults. It had to be even harder for the kids who knew Lori.

Carolyn herself had been devastated about Denise. She and Denise had played together as kids and went through school together. Although they had grown apart, they had always been on friendly terms. They would even stop in the aisles at the Piggly Wiggly to trade recipes or discuss teachers their children shared. Their deaths were a concept few could yet grasp.

As Carolyn stood at the window, Freddy broke the silence. "Thanks for the brownie. I've got to go help dad. And I promise, this isn't too much. This is good for me. I'm learning a lot and it's my way of helping poor Lori."

He stopped at Carolyn, gave her a quick kiss on the cheek and made his way past her. Trotting down the steps, he saw his dad shutting the building door.

"Hey, Freddy! I was just coming to find you. I've got to go downtown and try to find an appropriate wig for Lori. Wanna come along? You may be able to spot a closer match than I could."

Freddy nodded his head. He hadn't thought about the damage to Lori's head and scalp, but if the family wanted an open coffin, they would have to try to make her look as normal and lifelike as possible.

The drive into downtown only took five minutes. When they reached their destination, Freddy looked up at the sign. *Thomas Funeral Equipment and Supplies* hung in black, Goth letters above the door. It was also painted on the glass store front, but the sign above the door seemed more professional.

Fred jumped out as if he were on springs as Freddy hesitated momentarily. Fred looked back and saw that Freddy's mouth was moving.

"What's that, son?" Fred asked.

Freddy realized that he'd spoken aloud and quickly said, "I said that was a quick drive."

Fred just smiled and held the door for Freddy and they both stepped in together. What Freddy was really saying was *I don't want to think about that now. Just shut up!*

His inside-voice was telling him that it would be so funny if they chose a black wig to push down onto Lori's head. His inside voice was laughing hysterically.

Frickin' hilarious! That's what it'd be. Frickin' hilarious.

Freddy couldn't imagine why his inside-voice hated Lori so much more than he did. She wasn't overly friendly, but she wasn't really mean, either. She just kind of followed along with what the other kids were doing and saying—that was all.

"Hello, Fred," the soft-spoken man said.

Fred and his son had been here before and the owner, Hampton Thomas, was a colleague of Fred's. The two men shook hands and began to talk. Hampton shook his head in agreement with Fred as he told him what he needed.

Hampton acted like he already knew. Wadesboro was a small town and word usually traveled fast, especially about something like Lori's accident and death, so it was likely that he did already know what they were there for. He probably knew that most of Lori's hair was singed off leaving her bald. He probably knew about her ear, too.

As the two men walked along, the floor beneath them creaked in an almost eerily way. This building had been Thomas Funeral Supplies for twenty years and before that, it was Thomas Funeral Parlor. When Hampton's father passed away in 1950, Hampton was given an option. He could continue with the funeral home business, or make it something more.

Since his decision to make it something more, he had not only made much more money, he had offered something for his former rivals. Now, they came to him for supplies and equipment. He had business associates instead of rivals, and it felt good. Unless a funeral director ordered from a catalog, they came to him for all of their needs. And those associates came from many of the larger towns. He dealt with funeral directors from Albemarle, Monroe, Rockingham and even Charlotte.

Freddy just tagged along as Hampton pulled a curtain back and allowed him and his dad to walk on through. Before them stood an array of wigs, toupees, and assorted hair accessories. White Styrofoam heads stood on shelves and counters, each sporting some kind of hairpiece. And each hairpiece was adorned with a white price tag that swung back and forth in the slight breeze created as they walked along.

Fred looked down at his son. Freddy seemed totally enthralled by the scene. He never knew there was such a selection of hair to choose from.

"What do you think, son? Do any seem close to Lori's natural hair?"

Freddy walked on past several and when he saw the long, black wig before him, his inside-voice bellowed, *"Yeah, that's it, Fredlee! That's* it! *Pick that one. Let's see what they think of that!"*

Freddy ignored the constant voice and moved on quietly until at last, he saw the one. The one that looked just like Lori's hair when she wore it down on picture day. Blonde, but not too blonde. Not really sandy blonde, but almost yellow. Bright, sunny, and bouncy—just like Lori.

"Yes, sir. That's it." He pointed to the pretty wig.

Fred let out a whistle when he saw the price written on the tag. "I think we may need to find one that's not quite so, well, extravagant."

With that, Hampton offered another wig. It wasn't at *all* like Lori.

"Dad, that's not like Lori's hair. Not at all like Lori's."

"Well, son. Money is an obstacle. Mr. Eades isn't paying for one funeral, but two. I think this one will do just fine, Hamp."

Hampton nodded and smiled as he removed the wig from the white dummy head. Toting it back up near the front of the store, he began to write a sales ticket.

Freddy was angrier than he'd ever been. His inside-voice was laughing loudly.

Well, well, well. It might as well be black. That's just fine, Fredlee. It's not what's on the outside, is it? It's what's on the inside that counts, right? Oh, wait! There's nothing on the inside now!

The voice laughed loudly.

Freddy held his tongue until they were back in the car. Fred had also bought molding wax, Betco Facial Cream in light flesh tone and an ear mold. Freddy was furious.

"Dad, why did you buy that ugly wig for Lori? It's nothing at all like her own hair. This wig is almost red!"

Freddy pulled the disgusting thing from the paper bag that held the other supplies. Fred tried to explain to Freddy that this would have to do. Money was tight and Mr. Eades wasn't made of the stuff.

Freddy didn't care. Lori deserved better. His Lori deserved much better.

Your Lori? Your *Lori? What do you mean* your *Lori? She never even looked at you, Fredlee. She only noticed you when you were falling, tripping or stuttering. Would you listen to yourself? You are so pathetic! You do realize that, don't you?*

Freddy wanted to scream. He wanted to break into the supply store and take the wig that should be for Lori. He wanted to scream at his dad for giving in too easily. He wanted to scream for his inside-voice to shut up. He wanted to open the car door and jump out and start running. He wanted to do many things, but he just sat there, silently staring out the window and he felt a tear forming in the corner of his eye. He couldn't believe it, but he was crying for Lori Eades.

One Grave Secret

Chapter Seven

Freddy sat still and quiet for the remaining drive home. Traffic was backed up on Highway 74 near what locals referred to as 'The Curve'; it was a sharp, hairpin curve that curled around the perimeter of downtown. It was notorious for causing many accidents, some fatal, but mostly tractor-trailers that didn't calculate the sharpness of the curve well enough.

Mostly these were truckers not accustomed to the area, or the occasional beach bump-up as cars haphazardly slammed on brakes at the realization of just how sharp 'The Curve' was. As they sat waiting, Fred made some comment about hoping it was nothing fatal. The town couldn't handle another tragedy now and he just wasn't able to accommodate more visitations. Freddy barely noticed what his dad was saying.

His inside-voice was yakking away, telling him what a loser he was, and laughing at the comments he had made. Eventually, the voice was nothing more than a murmur, as if it was coming from under water. His eyes grew heavy and soon, Freddy was asleep.

He dreamed again. This time, he was in the building all alone. He walked to the drawer that held his sleeping beauty and tugged on the tray. As it slid out, Lori was wearing a long, black wig. Her lips were painted blood red, as were her long, pointed nails.

He couldn't help thinking, *why did dad do this?* ' But as he looked down at Lori in disgust, she opened her eyes quickly and sat straight up. She grabbed his hands and began to shout out "Come join me, Fredlee! Come on!"

Freddy tried to jerk away from her cold grip, but to no avail.

"Why are you doing this? What do you want?" he shouted.

Lori only smiled and very quietly, almost in a whisper, she answered him. "Because, Fredlee, this is the only way you'll ever have someone like me."

Lori lay down, crossed her hands over one another and closed her eyes again. The drawer began to pull away from him and his hands immediately flew back. As the drawer slammed shut, the handle pushed down, locked in place and Freddy woke up.

He was pouring sweat and trembling.

"Freddy? What's the matter, son? You okay?"

Freddy sat motionless as he realized he had only been dreaming.

"Sure dad, I'm fine."

Very soon after, they were turning into the bumpy gravel drive. Fred turned left and took the building drive. He didn't even have to ask his son if he wanted to help. He knew he did.

Fred was still talking about the costs of wigs and makeup when he unlocked the building door. Freddy was still angry with his dad. Actually, he was angry with Hampton Thomas. Why did he even show his dad a less expensive wig? Why was it bothering him so badly?

He needed to forget the whole thing before he lost control and was sent inside to help his mom or listen to records. No, he would keep it together. He had to, for Lori.

As he watched his dad work, Freddy sat silently on the stool. It too was stainless steel. This building looked like an operating room with all the bright lights and steel.

The only noise was the humming of the window unit air conditioners. The house wasn't cooled this way, not even the front rooms where visitation was held. Most of these rituals were held at night and it wasn't too bad after sunset.

When Fred dropped a pair of scissors, Freddy jumped. He was becoming more and more jumpy with each passing minute.

When this is all over, Fredlee, you'll be fine. This is just a minor setback. Cheer up, kiddo. Calm down and enjoy this moment. It's almost time. Can you feel the excitement? I can. I can't wait to get started!

Fred gently pulled the drawer out and Freddy helped his dad slide the tray from the freezer to the table. Freddy switched on the light just above where Lori lay. It was the kind of light on a swinging arm that resembled the same thing a dentist would use. In fact, Dr. Neal did have one like this. Freddy wondered, *Did Dr. Neal shop at Thomas Funeral Supplies and Equipment, too?* Dentist office, funeral parlor, it was about the same, wasn't it? Freddy smiled at that. It was a little funny to him, the comparison he made. He hated Dr. Neal's office. Every kid in Anson County did.

Because he had already cleaned the girl, this part, although time consuming, wasn't too hard. Freddy was very interested as his dad began to heat a hot plate. He'd seen it in the cabinet before, but never really wondered about what it was used for.

With the hot plate glowing warm, Fred took the molding wax from the packet he had purchased and slowly added it to a pan on the burner. As his dad stirred it slowly, Freddy watched as the wax became liquid.

He seldom asked questions, as he and his dad had realized that he learned more from just watching. Even though he wasn't sure what his dad was doing, he knew he'd know soon enough.

With the wax rolling in the pan, all warm and liquid, Fred asked Freddy to grab the ear mold from the bag. Freddy obliged, handing the box to him.

As Fred opened it, a metal box was revealed. Fred sprayed cooking oil in the mold, then poured in the wax and carefully closed the box. He gently set it on a side tray and looked to his son.

"Now you know what I'm doing, don't you?"

"Yes, sir. You just made a new ear for Lori."

Fred smiled. "That's right. A new ear for Lori."

As the ear was hardening, Fred took the Betco Facial Cream and began covering the multiple scars made by the Buick's windshield. When Fred began to hum his favorite song, Freddy felt a surge of relaxation.

He didn't even have to ask for permission before clicking *play* on the eight-track. The soothing sounds of Madame Butterfly began again and filled the room as it had many times before.

When Fred was done with the number two light flesh tone concealer, he softly added rosy pink in number three to Lori's cheeks. It made her look alive and healthy, just sleeping. Freddy liked that.

Then Fred opened the mold, revealing an almost real looking ear. Turning the mold over, the ear flopped out like a gelled desert into his hand. He painted on a special glue, and then firmly placed the ear into position.

This was getting better and better. Fred placed cotton inside her mouth to fill in her cheeks and sewed her mouth shut. Her eyeballs were covered with plastic cups and glued shut. The not so nice details were completed.

To see Lori come to life again was surprisingly pleasing. Apparently, his inside-voice was content with her transformation, too. It had remained quiet for several minutes now.

As Fred lowered the sheet, Freddy felt a little lump in his throat. He had never lowered any sheet that far before.

Sure, he'd seen plenty of naked corpses. But they were usually old bags that were so swiveled up and disgusting, he never even thought to look at them in a sexual way. But this was Lori Eades.

Her body was as perfect as a sixteen year old could be. Nothing like the pictures he'd seen in Allen's Muffler Shop or the calendar girls he'd seen in the back room of the barbershop.

He'd been back there only once, to use the bathroom, but seeing those women, all naked and smiling were what he assumed sexy was supposed to be. He thought about Mrs. Kate. *She* was sexy.

This was somehow different. This was Lori Eades and looking down at her now, he was sure what sexy was. He really liked what he saw.

Everything was almost done now. Fred reached behind him, pulling a machine up near Lori; the machine was on wheels, making it much more convenient to move about. He plugged an IV into Lori's abdomen and flipped a switch. As the machine began to shake a little, the contents inside started to slosh around. Within a few seconds, a formaldehyde, water, alcohol and glycerin solution flowed into Lori's body. As the liquid went in, Lori's natural liquids oozed out through a second tube. Soon, the only liquid Lori's body held was the embalming mixture.

Two hours had flown by when his dad's voice piped up. "Freddy, hand me the sack over there, will you?" Fred was nodding toward a bag from Moore and Sons Department Store. It contained the clothes that Mr. Eades had sent. These were the clothes Lori would be buried in. Freddy reached for the bag and noticed two dresses, both identical, but in different sizes. The smaller one was for Lori, the larger for her mother. They were to be buried in matching outfits.

Fred dressed Lori in the green floral print that looked like it was custom made just for her. The color seemed to make her look even more natural. As Fred continued, the eight track stopped, leaving them in silence, which was fine. They were both too consumed in what they were doing to notice.

Finally, Fred pulled a long, pink rose from the bag. It was artificial, but when Fred placed it in Lori's hands and folded them together, it looked simply beautiful. Stunning, in fact.

"Now, Freddy, I know you aren't happy with the wig we purchased, but it's time to put it on. It will be just fine, okay?" Freddy nodded and handed the dreadful thing over.

As Fred worked to place the wig in the right position, Freddy stepped back and realized that in this light, it was beautiful. He smiled as Fred looked up to him for approval. Freddy nodded and smiled as they both sat propped up on stools and examined their work. Lori Eades was finally ready for company.

After Lori was completely finished, the two Fred's together slid her back into the drawer where she would remain until the Eades family came to view and approve their daughter, sister, granddaughter and niece. Now, they would repeat much of the same process on Denise. Only Denise didn't need fake body parts, a wig or so much concealer. She just had to have the basic funeral parlor treatment. That's what Fred called it, The Basic Treatment. To Freddy, it was boring and uneventful, so he helped his dad do what he could, then left the building.

He made his way upstairs to his room, put on a record and sat up on his bed. It wasn't until Carolyn called him down for dinner that he ventured out from his room. This was his safe haven away from the bullies and jerks that made his life miserable.

Even though his inside-voice was amazingly quiet, he couldn't help but wonder why. What exactly had he done to please it?

During dinner that evening, the Lee family talked about the usual family dinner stuff. Nothing too important. Carolyn refused to hear about Fred's work at the table, but she did ask one thing, something that Freddy couldn't believe he hadn't thought of himself.

"When will visitation be, dear?" She really needed to know so that she could open the windows in the front rooms and let some of the staleness out. She would also clean the coffee pot, make sure they had plenty of the bitter stuff and dust and vacuum. Those were her main responsibilities in the family business.

"Tomorrow night from seven to nine for Denise, Thursday night for Lori, and I still don't know about Deacon Mills. I've done all I can, but unless a family member is found, I suppose it will be up to us to plan an hour of visitation, just in case."

The police department had run the plates on the truck he drove, but still no family had been found to identify the body. He would be buried at Memorial Cemetery. Memorial wasn't a potter's field, but in Anson County, there really wasn't a need for such. The one or two transients that had died in or near the county were buried there.

"Well, tomorrow I'll get busy tidying up in the front," Carolyn replied. It would be neat and clean for the Eades family and for Deacon Mills, whether he had family come or not. Carolyn was a hard worker and took great pride in all she did. Making things comfortable for Deacon's family would be no exception.

Fred patted his wife's hand and thanked her for a delicious meal. Then he and Freddy both excused themselves from the kitchen and went their separate ways. Fred, to the den to watch *Emergency!* as Freddy headed back upstairs to do his homework.

Visitation for Denise Eades was as smooth and pleasant as any visitation could be. Of course, there was the distraught family and Roger Eades was clearly devastated. The crying and sobbing were to be expected. Freddy had heard it all before.

Even though it was heartbreaking for most of them, Freddy had somehow grown immune to the racket. It was just white noise to him. He knew he should feel *something,* but he simply didn't. All he felt was an anxious gnawing in the pit of his stomach because tomorrow night, the house would be full of people that seemed to hate him.

Kids from school would come in and see him in his blue suit, complete with a rose pinned to the lapel. They would snicker and giggle at Fredlee, the boy who seemed to fail at everything. Only he had a secret.

He had already seen the mangled remains before they were tidied up. He had seen *all* of Lori Eades.

He had taken great pleasure in touching her soft, cold skin. He had done more than just touch her, too.

He had kissed her. He had allowed his fingers to dance around in places she had never been touched before. He had done the unthinkable, too. Yes, Freddy had made love to Lori. And he enjoyed every minute of the intense experience.

Lori liked it, too. He heard her moaning. He felt her writhing and begging for more.

Lori loved him. His inside-voice was wrong. She *did* love him and he would do anything to protect her from a harsh world that would never understand.

Chapter Eight

On Thursday, September 28, the weather conspired to provide the hottest night in Anson County to date. Clouds had begun to fill the late summer sky and a storm promised to bring cooler weather though.

At two thirty that afternoon, school was dismissed. Some of the younger kids that never knew Lori were just excited to be released thirty minutes early. Everyone began to make their way to cars, buses or sidewalks that led away from the schoolyard.

Freddy walked faster than usual. He wanted to spend some special time with Lori before the crowds gathered. As he headed up the drive, he noticed the hearse was out front, where his dad had left it the day before.

A long line of grieving mourners had followed in behind the hearse all the way to Restful Hills Cemetery, outside of Wadesboro, the previous day.

The line seemed to go on forever in the mirror Freddy gazed through. Over every hill, he could see the line of cars, bobbing up and down like a roller coaster. His dad drove the hearse, but he sat quietly in the passenger seat. The two family cars directly behind them were driven by Hampton Thomas and his son, Jimmy.

Freddy shied away from Jimmy as much as possible. But almost everyone did. Jimmy had been sent home three months earlier from Vietnam. He was recovering from an explosion that had left him deaf in one ear, limping on a bad leg, and he seemed to stare a little too long at anyone that got too close. Freddy had heard his mother whispering on the phone with his aunt Christine.

"Lord only knows what that poor boy endured over there. Bless his heart, he's just lost now. You be sure and keep Joe and Lynn away from him."

And he assumed that Robin had said the same thing on her end of the line.

"Yes, and make sure you keep Freddy away from him, too."

Freddy imagined what the passengers in that car were thinking. Probably, they were hoping they would end up at the graveyard alive and not down some dead end road where they would be executed. He thought how they were more than likely sweating through suits and dresses and nylons that made them all the more antsy. He smiled a little as he thought to himself, *better them than me.*

When the cars finally came to a stop and the doors slowly began to open, people filed around the open graves, one for Denise, and the other for Lori. They had both been dug already. A green tent covered the grave and gave some relief from the relentless sun. A darker green canvas tarp covered the grave where Lori would soon be placed. The tent above served to shade the whole area.

The preacher had spoken softly and kindly of Denise. He read from Revelation, how there will be no more tears someday. And then they all bowed their heads to pray. Everyone, except

Freddy. He looked around and saw that one other person wasn't praying, either. Jimmy Thomas stared at him with an ugly look that said, "I know what you did." But how could he? No one knew.

When the preacher finally said "amen", the family stood and began the usual hugging and shaking of hands. This was the boring part of a funeral director's job, standing and waiting for the event to finally come to an end.

When it did end, Fred, Carolyn and Freddy piled into two cars, leaving the one family car for Hampton to drive. Life was back to normal for today. Tomorrow would be the same thing all over again, but then it would be for Lori.

All of the memories from the day before raced through his mind as he trudged up the hill leading up the drive. Freddy walked into the house to find both his parents sitting at the table, sipping coffee and talking. They smiled and greeted him simultaneously.

"Hey, there, Freddy! How was school? Was it a little easier today?"

They waited for Freddy to nod and respond.

"Yeah, pretty much back to normal."

He helped himself to the cookie jar. As he leaned against the kitchen sink and ate his snack, his parents continued their conversation. It was boring stuff that didn't concern him in the slightest, so he grabbed a few more cookies and headed to the den. It was time for *Sanford and Son.*

He was dying to go see Lori, but knew that his parents would find it odd. He fought the urge as long as he could, but when he saw that there was no other time to go, he asked his dad as casually as he could.

"Dad? Do you think it would be okay for me to see Lori one last time? You know, before everyone else gets here? Just to say goodbye? I haven't done that yet. We were so busy preparing and I'd really like to do that."

Fred looked up from his place on the sofa in the living room. "Sure, Freddy. I think that would be fine. Want company?"

"Not really. I want to tell her goodbye and that might be hard with you there."

Fred completely understood his son's need to bid a farewell to his friend, so he allowed him to go alone.

Freddy stopped by the kitchen to grab the building key from a hook near the door. He hurried to the building as fast as he could. He hated to keep Lori waiting. They had not seen each other all day and he was really craving her undivided attention.

As he pulled her out again, he heard the first clap of thunder in the distance. But that didn't stop him or slow him down. He pulled up his stool and sat next to Lori for a few minutes, admiring her beauty.

He then carefully slid the pink rose out of her hands and stood next to her. She smiled at him and said, "Hey, Fredlee! I've been waiting for you! Come here, baby. I want something else in my hands now. That rose just wasn't doing it for me."

They both began to laugh as he unzipped his pants and gave her something else to grasp. Of course, she had to have some help holding things correctly, but that was to be understood. As the storm approached, the building grew darker.

"Perfect weather for us, huh?" Lori whispered in Freddy's ear.

He agreed. It was perfect, romantic even. For the next little while, they enjoyed a very sensual rendezvous together. He stroked her hair, apologizing for the cheap wig again. But she insisted it was fine. She loved the color. It was a change she had wanted, anyway.

After he had replaced her dress, the rose, and adjusted her wig, he gave her a quick peck on the forehead with a promise to see her again. Thank God, his inside-voice had been quiet all day. He could think so much clearer and his head didn't hurt. Lori seemed to be good for him. Of course she was. After all, they were made for each other.

As he walked around the corner, he almost ran into Roger Eades and his sons. They were just arriving for the final inspection of Lori's body. They were led into the den as Fred and Freddy rolled Lori out from the building in her silver coffin. The interior was pink, and Lori loved it. She assured Freddy that it really was perfect. Her father had picked it from a catalog and Hampton Thomas had delivered it this morning.

When the coffin was placed in just the right spot, Freddy switched on the awful pink lamps on either end. He rolled the coffin slightly to his left, making sure the lighting hit her beautiful face just right. As he stood there examining the last details, Lori winked at him. His heart skipped a beat as he realized that this was his girl and he was her man.

"Perfect. You look just perfect, Lori." Freddy smiled at her. She smiled back, and then closed her eyes.

Roger and her brothers were led into the parlor then and, of course, Roger just had to break down.

What was it with people? Why were they so emotional? He thought that he should be, too. But the only thing he felt was pride that Lori Eades loved him.

The storm lasted well into the night, even after visitation had ended and everyone had gone. Lori was escorted back to her drawer for the final time.

Fred thanked Freddy for all of his help and gave him a pat on the back. He was really proud of how professional his son was and how well he'd handled himself. He'd shown little emotion, which was good considering the fact that others were depending on them to hold it together. If the funeral director lost control of his emotions, the whole crowd might get hysterical.

Fred and Freddy made their way into the den to watch *I Love Lucy* and unwind for the night. Carolyn joined them and only mentioned the visitation once. She commented on how sweet and lifelike Lori had seemed and that her men had done a great job on both Denise and her daughter. She didn't have to tell Freddy. He knew how beautiful she was.

When the show they enjoyed went off, the three Lee's made their way to their bedrooms. Freddy stood just inside his door, waiting for his parents to fall asleep.

The storm was still howling and Fred Senior just could not rest with the flashes of lightening around. Every time he shut his eyes, there was another bright bolt, followed by a loud boom that jarred the windows. Carolyn slept sound as a baby with the rain hitting the roof and dotting the windowpanes. Freddy was in his room, pacing.

How long until he finally falls asleep? Just sleep, dad! Just go to sleep!

He was growing more and more anxious as he waited to see Lori. It had been six hours since he'd held her. He just didn't know how much longer he could wait. Finally, he heard the snoring he'd been waiting on and quietly crept down the stairs and out into the pouring rain.

He heard Lori calling him before he even got the door unlocked.

"I'm here, sweetie. I'm here now. I'm so sorry I couldn't get here sooner. I'm so sorry I left you alone. Did the storm scare you? The thunder is so loud."

Lori just grabbed him around the waist and clung tightly.

"You're here now. That's all that counts, darling. You're here now".

And all night they enjoyed touching, kissing, and loving each other, as they knew this was their last night together.

Thirty minutes before sunrise, Freddy said goodbye to Lori and silently slipped in through the kitchen. He walked ever so softly up to his room and snuggled down under his blanket, just as Carolyn opened his door to wake him.

Today, he would once again ride in the hearse with his dad to Restful Hills and look behind him at the cars following them. And just like yesterday, the preacher would read from the bible, pray, and solemnly console a devastated family.

Freddy was distraught, too. How on earth would he deal with this? He'd just found his one true love and now he was losing her. That grave was deep and dark. He just couldn't let his Lori lay there. He just couldn't do that. What *would* he do?

Chapter Nine

The night dragged on forever. Lori Eades was in her coffin, six feet underneath the soggy dirt, and Freddy couldn't get fixed. He tossed and turned and slid this way and that. Finally, when he could stand it no longer, he stood from his bed and walked over to his dresser.

He stared at the image looking back at him and was confused by what he saw. Freddy was no longer there. Instead, the inside-voice was shining through. He turned away, but the image in the mirror didn't. He looked back and gasped when his image looked away. His inside-voice couldn't stand to talk to him, let alone look at him. He was an utter disgrace.

Freddy paced the floor for an hour. The stillness of the humid air clung to the drapes, but didn't offer any relief from the heat. He made his way to the window, looking down at the building. It was almost empty again, except for Deacon Mills. No reason to go down there. No reason to even live now.

He considered getting the revolver from Fred's gun safe and blowing his brains out right there. He thought about taking all the painkillers in the medicine cabinet. They were there to help Carolyn cope with the migraines that plagued her. He opened his closet and considered looping a belt tightly around his neck. The only thing that kept him from ending it all was a promise he had made to Lori.

Earlier that day, as they held each other tightly, Lori talked to Freddy.

"I know it will be hard, Fredlee, but you have to try. You have to stay strong, baby."

Freddy shook his head and held her sweet, frozen hand in his. He tried to remain strong, tried to be brave, but he knew that it would be hard to accept. He just never knew how hard it would be.

When his inside-voice began, it was a welcome sound. He needed to know what to do and how to handle this whole messed up situation.

Fredlee. Think about it. Will you just think about it? You could go and dig the bitch up. But that would take a helluva lot of time and effort. Is she even worth it? I tell you what to do. Find another Lori. Basically, Fredlee, they're all the same. They all want the same things and they all have the same things. Just go shop around. You can drive, can't you? Take the car, drive around and find Lori. Your *Lori.*

Freddy eased down onto his bed. The idea wasn't really that farfetched. Considering the lengths he'd already gone to, it wasn't a terrible notion. He thought about how he could go about bringing Lori home and with a lot of brainstorming, he and his inside-voice had the plan perfected.

* * * * * * *

The next morning, Freddy walked around the perimeter of his dad's building. Fred had gone downtown to restock supplies and Carolyn was at the hair salon. She went every three days, so no surprises there.

He still walked into the building precariously. If his dad should come home and catch him, he'd have a lot of explaining to do. But there was something in there he needed. His inside-voice had given him very clear instructions.

Use detrepanol, Fredlee. You know what it does. You can bring Lori home easy breezy with that junk.

Freddy did know what detrepanol was. Fred used it sometimes to soften thick muscle tissue. It also helped relax stiff joints. One small injection was really all a corpse needed. It wasn't used often, but Fred kept a vial or two, just in case it was needed in an instant. Freddy had read the label once before out of boredom coming home from Thomas Supplies.

Warning: this drug can cause serious health problems if ingested. If you are subjected to internal use, seek professional help immediately. Do not call poison control. Seek emergency care at once. Symptoms may include, but are not limited to lethargy, comatose state, headaches, dizziness, and death.

Under the warning label was a skull and crossbones.

Freddy had placed the vials in a cabinet and then gone about helping his dad. To his knowledge, the bottles were still there. If they weren't, he'd have to rethink his whole plan. When he opened the cabinet, they were gone. He continued to search and found them behind some syringes, tubes, and hoses.

Perfect, Fredlee! Perfect. Now, grow a pair and go get your Lori!

Freddy smiled as he listened to his inside-voice. Oh, he had a pair and he was soon going to prove it. He slipped the vial and a syringe into his jacket pocket and casually strolled out of the building. He'd have to take the car again, but he was pretty sure he could get away with it.

It was the weekend and the kids from school were bound to be out later. He had laughed at his parents for going to bed so early before, but now he was glad of it. He would require privacy soon.

When Fred and Carolyn had said goodnight to their son, they headed up stairs, hand in hand. The idea of what might be on their mind sickened him.

"I'm going to watch *The Brady Bunch*. I'll go to bed soon," Freddy responded.

He waited an hour and a half, plenty of time he hoped, before sneaking up to check on his parents. They were sound asleep, just as he had expected.

He got dressed in his best light blue leisure suit, slicked his hair back just a little and slipped into his white dress shoes.

Shit, Fredlee. You look like a frickin disco king. Really. You really do disgust me.

His reflection turned to go before he was spinning around to leave. That really bothered him. He couldn't quite make that out. But he was ignoring the voice, either way.

He cruised around a little before heading to *Roller Rinker's*, the local hangout for teens. As he turned into the parking lot, he saw several kids from school walking into the building while others were leaving. He pulled in and smoothly parked the car. From here, he could see the bright, spinning lights of a disco ball shining through the darkness. Reflections sparkled on the dashboard like diamonds, and he could hear the thumping of the music pounding away inside. He really didn't want to go in. He was hoping he could find Lori from here.

He didn't think anyone would recognize him. After all, he'd never been here. This place was way out of his league. There wasn't a girl within twenty miles that would give him the time of day, except for his Lori. That was all he could think about now. He just had to find her and quick. He had a time bomb in his pants ready to explode. He missed her sweet touch, her smell, her breath on his neck.

As he sat there thinking about everything they had shared, he heard her.

It was Lori!

She was walking into Roller Rinker's with some other girls he didn't recognize. He jumped out of the car and headed directly to her.

"Lori! Hey, Lori!" Freddy yelled.

The girls kept talking, ignoring Freddy. The door slammed shut in his face. He felt anger replacing his solitude. He turned, ready to go home defeated when he saw a beautiful girl, almost as pretty as Lori.

She had long, flowing red hair that shone bright under the neon skating sign.

Damn, Fredlee! That's her! *That is Lori! The hair color doesn't matter, remember? Get her. Get her now!*

Fredlee walked up behind Lori as she walked past him.

"Lori, I've missed you so much!" Freddy said. His voice was almost inaudible. He could feel himself quivering under the polyester suit.

The red headed girl turned to him. "Sorry, I guess you thought I was someone else, huh?"

"Yeah, I guess so. Sorry."

Lori smiled sweetly. "That's okay. I'm Erin. And who are you? I don't think I've ever seen you here before, have I?"

"Um, no. I just moved here." Freddy couldn't believe she didn't know him.

"Well, I'm here visiting my cousin. She's inside. Come on!" Erin opened the door and the loud music spilled out.

"I left my skates in my car. Come with me to get them?"

Erin stood for a moment and thought about that. Then she shrugged her shoulders. "Sure. Why not?"

Freddy smiled and held out his hand. The two walked towards the Impala together without speaking. When they reached the car, Freddy unlocked the door and bent down. He felt the vial in his hand and quickly removed the cover from the needle. He pumped the syringe to spew out just a little of the detrepanol.

"Do you have them?" Erin asked. She was bouncing just a little as she stood there with her arms crossed. "Cause my cousin, Libby is waiting".

"I have them right here," Freddy said smoothly. As he turned, he plunged the needle into her neck.

He loved the look of total surprise in Lori's eyes as the needle penetrated her delicate skin. She jerked briefly and then fell limp in Freddy's arms. He looked around cautiously and saw a couple walking towards him.

You better think of something lightning fast, Fredlee.

His inside-voice had a way of helping him think faster sometimes. He leaned in and began to kiss "Lori" on the mouth. The couple walked right on by and the man gave a little whistle towards Freddy.

The taste on Erin's lips was repulsive to him. He hated her almost immediately. This was not Lori. This was *not* Lori. He pushed her in from the driver's side and slid her across the wide seat.

Don't forget to lock her in, Fredlee. She'll wake up and try her damnedest to get out.

Freddy didn't think to do it, so he was glad his inside-voice had reminded him. Freddy reached over and popped the lock on the door. The little knob was just even with the door. If she did wake up, she could still get out. He had to hurry and get home.

Erin did wake up, unfortunately about five minutes too late. They were pulling in the driveway when her eyes cracked open. She was so dazed and her limbs felt heavy. She tried to reach up to rub her pounding head, but she couldn't get her arms to work.

"Good morning, sleeping beauty," Freddy whispered. Erin didn't hear him. She was already trying to escape.

"It will be much easier if you don't fight it. Trust me. I don't want to hurt you, Lori."

"But, I'm not Lori. My name is Erin. Erin Underhill. I told you already," She said, sluggishly.

"Don't smart mouth me, bitch. I don't care what you call yourself. You are going to be Lori."

Erin sank down into the vinyl of the seat. Tears were stinging her eyes. "Let me go. I'll do whatever you want. Just please, let me go. Please?"

Freddy smiled. He liked the panic in her voice. The submissive quality to her plea was so sexy.

"See, you are Lori. There's really nothing you can do about that. But, while you are here, you can make this much easier for yourself."

When he brought the car to a stop, he looked over at her. She was crying and sobbing now and her body was jerking involuntarily as she tried to regain her muscle motor function. He wasn't sure if that was terror or the detrepanol, but either way, she was quivering violently and it excited him.

"Calm down. We're home now, baby! You're finally home."

It took all of her strength, but she found a scream deep inside her and let it out full force. Freddy really didn't want to hurt Lori, but he had no choice. His inside-voice was screaming even louder.

"Shut her up, Fredlee. Do it. Make her stop or she'll ruin everything!"

Freddy reached across the seat and pulled Erin closer to him, looking her right in the eyes.

"You need to stop. I don't want to do it, but I will shut you up if you can't get a grip."

Freddy was as smooth and calm as he'd ever been. His inside-voice was very proud.

"Okay. Okay," Erin whimpered.

"That's a good girl. Lori would never be upset. I expect better of you."

He opened the car door and pulled her by her hair until she was standing next to him. She looked around, thinking she would need to be able to recall all the details she could. Her head was throbbing now, worse since Freddy had pulled with such force.

"Come on," he said sternly.

He held onto her tightly as they entered the building.

Work fast, Fredlee. Your daddy could come in at any minute. And then what would you do?

In his panic, he hadn't thought of that. Well, one thing at the time. He immediately had Erin lie down on the steel table centered in the middle of the room.

"If you move, I'll kill you. If you try to run, I'll find you. And believe me, my wrath will make you wish you were never born, Lori."

"I'm not Lori. I'm Erin. Please, please let me go."

Freddy laughed. He turned on the eight-track and stood still as the opera quietly began. He knew he had to keep the noise to a minimal now in order to maintain his privacy. He closed his eyes and imagined that the music was just for him. He felt a surge of power that he didn't know he had. Erin continued to sob.

"Lori, dear. You're ruining this moment. I'm going to make you a work of art. You are going to be a masterpiece! Relax and enjoy it. You'll be so beautiful when I'm done."

"What are you going to do to me?" Erin squeaked. Her voice was almost lost.

Freddy placed a thick string of cloth around her face and drew it firmly around her mouth. Then he added more cloth on top of that. She wouldn't scream now.

Next, he tied her down so that her hands were connected from underneath the table with a nylon rope. Her feet were left free. She couldn't escape, so there was really no need to bind them. Freddy patted her head as he walked around to the far end of the building. He reached for the tools he needed.

Erin's eyes grew wide as he pulled out the scissors. Freddy just laughed. He was amazed at the control he had now. He began to slowly cut her long, red hair. It fell to the floor in dreamy, wispy tendrils. When it was short enough, he opened the razor. He methodically began to shave her scalp. He could see Lori emerging already. When her head was slick, he smiled at her.

"You see? That didn't hurt one bit, did it?"

Erin had tears streaming down her face, but shook her head "no". Maybe by being obedient, she would survive whatever he was planning to do to her.

"That's a good girl, Lori."

Erin had given up on trying to convince him that she wasn't Lori. She quit trying to break free from the restraint of the rope, too. She just lay there helpless and terrified, praying that it would all be over soon.

Freddy stood back and looked at his handiwork. He had done okay, but he wasn't finished. He was just getting started, in fact. He wiped the razor down with alcohol, more out of habit than necessity.

"Now, I'll go ahead and warn you, Lori. You won't like what I have to do next. But trust me, you'll be so glad I did it when I'm done. Then you'll see that you *are* Lori."

Freddy's inside-voice was apparently content with his actions. It had remained quiet for several minutes now. The razor went over to the right side of Erin's head. With one fast movement, Freddy had taken off her right ear. Erin let out a dull, incomprehensible noise. In his warped mind, Freddy thought that the sound was a moan of pleasure.

"Well, I didn't think you'd like that. Apparently I was mistaken. You look beautiful, by the way."

He bent down to give her a kiss. "Nope. Still not there. But don't you worry. I'll have you perfect soon, baby. I promise."

Freddy rolled the machine by Erin as she watched on, beginning to go in to shock now.

"Just a little stick now. I'm sorry about that."

Freddy unbuttoned the front panel of Erin's pants. He pulled them down just enough to see the white flesh of her belly. He gave it a little thump.

"You're ripe, chick," Freddy teased.

Erin was in and out of consciousness now. When the fat needle plunged into her stomach, her eyes widened in pain and fear. Freddy flipped the switch and listened as the equipment began to hum. The solution inside began to slosh around and within ten seconds, was trickling in through the tube and making its way inside Erin.

"This will take two, maybe three hours. When we're done, I'll store you in the freezer drawer. You'll be fine, my sweet. Just relax. Don't fight it. It won't make any difference now. Thank you, Lori, for your help in making this precious masterpiece. It was a pleasure working with you."

Erin's eyes began to cloud over and before Freddy could finish his sentence, the formaldehyde was stinging every inch of her body. The pain was too much and she was already bleeding heavily from her detached ear.

Her head moved once, up toward the ceiling. Her back arched and then relaxed. She very briefly saw her own bodily fluids rushing through the tube and knew what was happening. Just before she died, she knew that her death was imminent.

Freddy watched as Erin drew her last breath. It was the most beautiful thing he'd ever seen. His inside-voice was still and quiet. He knew that it was also well pleased.

As soon as the process was complete, he unhooked Erin from the embalming machine and cleaned up all of his equipment. Then he lovingly slid Erin from the worktable to a shiny rolling stretcher as he had so many times before. Rolling her from the work area to the drawer section, he heard her speak.

"Oh, Freddy, why didn't you do this sooner? I feel so much better!"

Freddy smiled down at his lovely Lori.

"What did I tell you?"

"I need you, baby. It's been way too long," he heard Lori purr. That's what she sounded like—a cat purring and begging for him.

"Are you up for it? I know you've been through a lot and it's been a long day."

"Yes, of course I'm up for it. This is what I've been waiting for!" Lori began to writhe up and down as Freddy began to undress.

"I love you so much, Lori."

Freddy thought he really loved her. This was his only way to feel love and he had grown quite comfortable with the situation. Lori was so much more affectionate and submissive this way. Only a few minutes passed and Freddy was satisfied. Lori was happy to be here. If it lasted all night, that was wonderful. If their special time together was brief, that was good, too.

It was the closeness and warmth that she craved. Freddy believed every word she whispered as he held her. Soon, he stood and stared down at Lori. She was a special lady and he was so proud to have her back.

The clothes that Erin had worn were a little messy, so Freddy gently covered her with a crisp, fresh sheet and slid her into her drawer.

"I'll find you something special to wear tomorrow, sweetie. Now, you rest and I'll see you again real soon."

"Goodnight, my love," Lori said. "And thank you for being so kind to me. I've needed someone like you in my life, Fredlee."

Freddy gave the drawer a final push and listened as the air sealed in around Lori. He smiled to himself as he made his way to his bed. He finally slept a dreamless, peaceful sleep. He would have to do this more often. It was so good to rest and have quiet inside his mind. His inside-voice slept as well.

Chapter Ten

Freddy had driven the Impala before, but mostly around the driveway, just practicing. When Fred saw that the car wasn't exactly where he'd left it, he became a little more than curious. He walked around the side, then to the back of the car. He stood there puzzled, and then shrugged his shoulders. He had work to do in the building.

He was just pulling the drawer toward him when Freddy walked in.

"What are you doing, dad?"

Fred looked up and smiled at his son.

"You scared me, Freddy. I didn't hear you walking up. Just cleaning everything today. The last few days have been busy and I really need to take some time in the cleanup and maintenance department."

"I'll help. Here, I'll do that. Why don't you go and help mom. I think I heard her say something about you needing to cut the grass."

Fred stopped pulling and looked at his son.

"No, I don't think so. I cut the lawn yesterday."

Freddy could feel his pulse pounding against his temple. He was growing pale and clammy.

"Freddy? Are you okay? What's wrong, son?"

Freddy didn't move or speak. He was completely numb. He had hoped he could find somewhere else for Lori to sleep before this kind of problem arose. His inside-voice was silent, too.

"Freddy? Cat got your tongue?" As he spoke, he continued pulling the drawer out near to him. He stood looking down at Lori in complete confusion.

Although Freddy really didn't feel love toward his parents, he did have a profound respect for them. He never thought he would be forced to do the unspeakable. He knew his mom would be crushed without her soul mate, but there was really nothing Freddy could do except kill the one person who knew his secret.

He couldn't accept his father knowing. He walked nonchalantly to the cabinet where the detrepanol was stored, pulled out the last vial and pumped out the air from inside a syringe after he quickly filled it. When the medicine came spewing out, he looked up and saw Fred still standing there, looking down on Lori.

"Son? Freddy? Who is this? Why is she here?"

"Dad, this is Lori. Lori, please say hello to my father."

Fred was too stunned to even know how to respond. Freddy leaned forward, as if he meant to hug his dad. Confused, Fred leaned in closer to his son. Freddy raised the vial up behind his father and plunged it quickly into his carotid artery. Freddy spoke softly into his dad's ear.

"I really never thought this would happen. Dad, I'm sorry. Well, that's what I'm supposed to say, isn't it?"

Fred tried to speak, but his words were already slurring and beyond comprehension.

"What's that, Fred? I'm sorry. I couldn't hear you."

Fred didn't know what he was trying to say. He was thinking about Carolyn. Freddy sensed it and commented.

"This will be hard on mom, but I promise, I'll take good care of her for you, dad. Now, I'm thinking that what we should do now is maybe, well, I don't know. Strangulation? No. That would be questionable. I can't leave any identifying marks. Stroke? That's the cause of death. I'll make sure everyone knows you had a stroke. I'll give you just the right combination of detrepanol and glycerin. No one will ever know, will they?"

Freddy let Fred slide down onto the floor. He reached back into the cabinet and found the glycerin. It was housed in the same area. They used it in the mixture for embalming and Freddy knew all about the chemicals they had around. Fred thought that the science of their work was important, especially with Freddy leaving for college soon. Freddy was glad now that he had been so thoughtful toward his education.

As he pulled off Fred's shoe and slid the black sock from his foot, Fred tried to ask why, but what came out was more like the slur of a rambling drunk asking for one more for the road. Freddy laughed as his dad tried to make sounds and words. He put the needle between two toes, injecting the fatal dose, and quickly slid the sock back on. As he tied his dad's shoe, he watched as Fred struggled for air.

Fred Lee died within one full minute. Freddy stood, slid the drawer shut and looked around. Seeing a tray full of tools nearby, Freddy used his forearm to knock the tray clean. He overturned a stool for good measure and then began to yell wildly.

"Oh, God! Dad! Daddy!"

Carolyn was in the kitchen when she heard Freddy screaming. She quickly dried her hands and dropped the dishtowel as she ran from the house.

"Freddy? What on earth is the matter? Freddy?"

When she entered the building, she saw her husband sprawled on the floor, his right eye pulled down closer to his jawbone than his eyelid. His whole right side was pulled tightly down around the edge of his head.

"Fred! Oh my God, Fred!" Carolyn screamed out.

"Do something, Freddy! Do something!"

Freddy grabbed his mom and held her tightly.

"Mom, there's nothing that can be done. He's gone. I heard the tools hit the floor and when he didn't answer me, I came inside to check on him. He was gone before he hit the floor, mom."

Carolyn cried loudly and moaned with grief. Freddy whispered to her.

"I think we should take him inside, mom. Let's give him that dignity."

Carolyn shook her head in agreement. She was totally shocked and would probably need something to help her get through this. But for now, Freddy just wanted everyone out of the building.

No need for medical examiners or policemen in here rambling where they didn't belong. Inside, he could be just as dead. Inside and away from his secret.

* * * * * * *

It would be the hardest thing Carolyn would face, but having Fred home for his wake was comforting. Freddy took careful consideration in all the details. When it was all said and done, Fred Lee Senior was peacefully resting in his coffin in the front room of the Lee home and no one was the wiser.

Chapter Eleven

Freddy continued to do what he could to keep the business going, but until he had his degree in science and his state examiners license, his work was limited. He stayed on top of the latest information and equipment by reading *In the Way* magazine. He comforted Carolyn and tried to finish school.

The year couldn't have been slower dragging on, but at last, in June of 1974, Freddy walked across the stage of Bowman High School and received his diploma. Carolyn applauded proudly as her son shook hands with Mr. Richardson.

Freddy was proud, too, but momentarily, he had other concerns. Lori was at home, but still hiding in the building. He visited her nightly and promised that soon, she would be able to live in his room with him. He just wasn't sure what he would do. He would be away from home at college and leaving Lori behind wasn't an option he cared to weigh.

That night, Carolyn prepared her son's favorite dinner and the two of them sat quietly eating at the table. Carolyn stared through Freddy as he chewed. It was a look he'd grown used to, but since his father's death, it was becoming an almost daily event.

"Mom?" Freddy asked. He knew his mom wouldn't answer.

Eventually, Carolyn picked up her fork and continued eating.

You sorry, boy. That's all you are, you know? A little boy. You can't do anything without my help. I know you want Lori in here celebrating with you. Go get her, little boy. Drag her in here and plop her down right beside your mother. She's just a little gone now, Fredlee. In case you hadn't noticed, your mom is just about gone.

He took a bite from his roast beef and looked to his mother. The voice was right. His mom was slipping faster each day. Would she even know the difference if he just brought Lori in and introduced her?

His voice began laughing. *Can you imagine, Fredlee? I bet Lori would have more to say than your mom. I just bet your mom would try to shake her cold stiff hand!*

Freddy didn't want anyone to talk about Lori that way. He did consider what it was saying, though. There was no way he could bring Lori in. And no way could he leave her here this fall. He had three months to figure it out. Until then, he would just have to entertain the fact that Lori was lonesome and his mom was losing it. He finished his meal and excused himself.

When he pulled Lori out again, she was full of the same ideas and thoughts. He couldn't even enjoy her company tonight.

"What's wrong, baby?" Freddy asked himself, using a high-pitched tone to mock his lover.

"I'm torn, Lori. I'm finally through with school. But if I want to earn a degree and continue in the family business, I have to go to college. That means I'll be gone a lot. What if someone finds you while I'm away?"

Lori was silent and then Freddy imagined a bright smile sweeping over her face.

"I know! I know what to do, Freddy. Why not commute to school? It would be hard, but at least you'd be back each night. And maybe you could find me a friend to keep me company during the day? Someone just like me to talk to and enjoy."

Freddy couldn't believe how clearly that thought came to her. He smiled at her as she hugged him tighter.

"You are so good for me, you know that? We are perfect together. That is a wonderful idea and the perfect solution!"

Freddy pulled Lori's arms around him as tightly as he could. He loved the way she held him. "Friday, I'll go shopping. I'll find you the perfect friend. I promise, I'll make this work."

He held Lori a little while longer and when the sun began to rise, he rolled his lovely Lori back in to her drawer and locked up. He took the stairs up to his room and slid down under the covers. He knew that someday, Lori would be able to sleep right next to him.

* * * * * * *

Freddy was so excited. Not only was it Friday, it meant shopping day. He was out to find Lori a friend. This was a day he had anticipated all week.

"Don't you worry, baby. I'm bringing you home a friend today," Freddy had said, comforting her.

Here he sat waiting, wondering what lucky woman he'd find. He knew the roller rink wasn't a good idea. Friends, family and police were still searching for Erin Underhill. No, he needed a new place today. His inside-voice had not only reminded him to keep away from Roller Rinker's, it had helped him understand that he had to keep a low profile.

"Don't let the man see you walking around talking to girls, Fredlee. They don't need to concern themselves with our business."

As he began his search, he kept quiet and incognito. He had rambled through the drawers and cabinets in the building and found a short, black wig. It was one his dad had purchased for Mrs. Linsby, the lady from Lilesville who'd died of cancer.

The treatments she had tried caused hair loss. When her daughter saw her lying in that coffin with the unnatural hairpiece, she vied for a pretty scarf instead. Fred tucked the wig away, thinking he might use it later on another client, as he called the corpses he had worked on.

Freddy wore it now, along with one of his mother's dress he'd found hanging near the back of the closet. He assumed it was one she didn't wear or wouldn't miss. He found walking in the heels to be quite a challenge. He would never understand why women wore these things. He chose a pair of flat pumps instead, just in case he needed to run to get away. He made that connection all by himself, without his inside-voice piping up to tell him.

He stood in the bathroom, admiring himself in the mirror. He had to say he looked quite convincing. He twirled around and practiced his walk in a small circle until he was confident that he would pass as a woman.

Now, he was casually walking into the Hampton B. Allen library, a place he never came. No one should recognize him here.

"Can I help you, ma'am?" the librarian asked.

Freddy felt his heart beating harder when he realized the lady was talking to him. Using Lori's voice he answered, "Just looking for a good weekend read, that's all. I'm fine. But thanks for asking."

He smiled at her and he felt the lip color sliding around on his lips. It felt strange, but nice, too. He kind of liked the way it felt to be a girl.

He had only been in the library for around fifteen minutes when he saw her. Tall, blonde, and otherwise way out of reach. Freddy knew that as a man, she would never have given him the time of day, but this was different and he had a plan.

He grabbed a few novels from the shelf and sat three tables down from her. He watched casually as she made her way from one shelf to another, and then eased into the wooden chair. He continued to observe her as she stood again, walked to the reference section, fingered her way down the stack and pulled the book she was searching for out.

He glanced at her occasionally and two hours later, when he saw her going to the bathroom, he gracefully left the building.

He stood in the parking lot waiting, when finally she started toward a Volkswagen Beetle.

"Excuse, me, honey?" he chimed in a sweet feminine way.

"Yes?" the blonde responded.

He had the detrepanol in his sweater pocket, open and ready. The blonde was already making her way toward him.

"I've misplaced my glasses and I can't see well without them. It seems I dropped my keys around here somewhere and I can't find it. Would you be willing to help an old lady out?"

The blonde giggled. "Well, you're not old, but sure, I'll help you. Where were you standing when you dropped your keys?"

She was bending down, which was perfect. Freddy pulled the syringe from his pocket and pushed it into her back.

That was excellent, cat! he heard his inside-voice whisper.

Using his own manly voice, he answered her. "It was right there, honey."

The blonde started to scream, but Freddy stopped her.

"No, no, no. If you scream, I'll kill you right here. I'm going to open my door and you're going to get in. Understand?"

The blonde shook her head, fear streaming through her facial features.

"Good girl. That's a good girl."

Freddy opened the door, which was already unlocked. The blonde slid in and over and immediately reached for the passenger side door.

"Don't be stupid," he mumbled.

"I've already taken all the necessary precautions. No one will see us or know what's up. Don't worry."

"I'm," she started, and then the blonde began to nod. She fought the urge to sleep, but couldn't finish her sentence. She sat there with heavy eyes and realized that she could no longer move.

She struggled to speak, but the words came out all wrong.

"Lev not, no see wa—"

She was confused by how she sounded. She knew she had to get out and run away—scream or do something—but there was nothing she could do. Nothing she could say and then everything grew dark around her.

Freddy waited until they were on his street to remove the wig. Under Carolyn's dress, he wore his jeans and a thin shirt. He unzipped the flimsy thing and pulled it over his head.

The flats came off, too. He spread his toes in relief as they again could move. He hadn't' worried about bringing extra shoes.

"Here we are, Beautiful! Home again, home again jiggidy jog!"

The blonde couldn't open her eyes completely, but stared through tiny slits as he pulled into the drive.

Freddy opened the door and dragged her out by her hair, just as he had done with Erin. No need to fix what isn't broken. She was beginning to struggle, but he was stronger. He never even looked at her. She really wasn't important to him, but she would be to Lori. This was a gift for her.

When they entered the building, he told her to get up on the table. She half stood, half leaned on him and started shaking her head.

"Get on the table, now!" Freddy yelled.

"No, please, no," the blonde tried to say. Instead, it sounded like *noplenno*.

Freddy rolled his eyes. He picked her up and sat her down on the worktable and with one quick movement, gave her another shot of detrepanol. The fog took over and when she came to again, she was gazing at a weird looking machine that made a loud, disgusting sound as liquid sloshed around inside.

What is this? Where am I? Who are you? she wanted to ask, but through the drug-induced haze, she could only lay there helplessly, watching Freddy.

"Oh, good. You're awake. I wanted to tell you about why you're here. You see, my girlfriend, Lori, is lonely. She needs a friend to keep her company while I'm at school. You are very fortunate that I chose you. Any girl would love to befriend her. She is very sweet and you'll love her. So, what's your name?"

Freddy stood waiting for the woman to respond.

"My name is Trish. Trish Colbert. I have—"

Freddy didn't wait for her to finish before interrupting her.

"Anyway, Trish, you'll be glad to know that not only are you going to be a best friend to Lori, I'm going to turn you into a genuine piece of art."

Trish lay still, listening. She was an intelligent girl, second in her class at Winhill Law. She was a junior and had worked all summer for a local law firm. She was heading back to school on Monday. The research she had done in the library today was to help a fellow classmate with too many classes and a full time job. She'd felt sorry for him and agreed to help him through the weekend. She was at the library because she wanted to help a friend. She was in the wrong place at the wrong time, she thought as she listened to Freddy ramble on and on about Lori.

"Can I meet her, your girlfriend? Maybe she and I can talk awhile and get to know each other."

Trish was doing what she had read about in the event of an attack or kidnapping in *Law and Crime* magazine last month. Anything to keep the assailant calm. Keep him talking, try to connect and make yourself seem human, and hopefully find an escape during the process.

"Why yes, you can meet her. I'm glad you're as excited to meet her as she is you." Freddy smiled down at Trish. "I just have to do one thing first. Now, you won't like what I have to do, but you see, Lori was in a bit of an accident recently and she lost her hair."

Freddy continued to talk as he began cutting Trish's hair. She lay thinking that she could always grow her hair back out. That wasn't such a big deal.

Let him cut it, Trish. Just let him cut it and when he turns around, you run! You run and scream and do whatever you must to get away! she was thinking.

After Freddy had shaved her smoothly, he rubbed her head. "Now, Lori won't feel so self-conscious. You did a great job, Trish."

And as he talked to her, Trish began to relax. That was a mistake because her guard was down. As soon as he came around to her left, she knew that.

The razor sliced so quickly, she didn't have time to do anything. He held her right ear up in front of her. It should have hurt terribly, but it didn't. Trish couldn't believe that it was her ear flapping in front of her. She lifted a hand to where her ear should be, feeling a gaping hole and smelling the metallic bloody odor on her hand.

"I avoided telling you about that part because when I cut Lori's off, she really had a hard time dealing with it. But don't you worry, Trish. Now you're beginning to look just like her."

Freddy was so pleased with his work. He inched back and looked at her.

"Beautiful, Trish. You are absolutely beautiful. Now, for the last step. I'll warn you. It might not be so pleasant, but you'll be so glad when we're all done. You'll be Lori's twin. And she'll love you!"

"Please don't rape me. I'll do anything you want. Please, just don't rape me."

Trish knew that she couldn't handle that. She had worked with rape victims in her sophomore year and dealt with all the harsh realities of life after rape. Talking to those poor victims had bothered her so much, they filled her dreams to this very day.

"Oh, Trish, that's disgusting. I would never do that. I only have eyes for Lori. And believe me, you are not my type. Not yet, anyway. But I still could never do that to anyone, ever."

Trish felt relief sweep over her. Maybe this freak just wanted her slightly mangled. Maybe now he was done and she could get Lori and get out of here. Then she felt him tugging on her pants.

"But you said—" she started and then she saw the needle. She wasn't sure what it was, but it was attached to a large tube and fed into a bucket of some sort. The bucket was clear and contained some kind of liquid.

She tried to scream, but Freddy covered her mouth. She bit down on him with all the strength she could muster. Freddy banged her head onto the table and when she let go of his hand pulled back, examining the wound.

"You stupid bitch!" But even with the injured hand, he had a job to do. "Lay still. This won't hurt as badly if you'll just lay still!" Freddy barked.

Trish had no intention of laying still. She pulled herself off the table and was racing for the door as Freddy was turning to pull the embalming machine to her. Blood spewed from the right side of her head, where her ear should be. It was beginning to throb now. She was regaining muscle control, which was good, but she was also starting to feel pain.

Freddy turned on the water to wash his hand. As soon as his mind was preoccupied, she jerked the heavy door open, and suddenly she was in the darkness of the night. She ran as fast as she could, down the pebble drive.

Don't look back, Trish, don't look back. Just run!

Freddy was running now, too. He was faster than Trish and didn't have the detrepanol in his system. She was at the end of the drive when Freddy caught her. She began to scream uncontrollably, her arms flailing this way and that, crying and kicking all at once. She thought she saw a light flip on in the house across the street, but everything was happening so fast, she didn't have time to look back again.

"Please! Help me! Somebody help me!" Trish continued wailing.

Freddy grabbed her by the neck and pushed down on her with all of his weight. She couldn't breathe now and was losing her battle.

She felt around on the ground, searching for a rock or anything to use as a weapon, but she found nothing. Her fingers continued to search, even after Freddy began to grow darker and darker.

She struggled for air, but none would come. She had fought a good fight, but she knew she had lost. Finally, she quit moving. Freddy knew the very moment Trish died. He could see it in her eyes. The blankness that emerged was one he had seen many times before. He pushed himself away, landing a few feet from Trish's still body. He had never felt so irate and defeated.

You loser! I knew you'd eventually fail. What are you going to do now, you stupid freak? What now?

Freddy sat for moment longer. He had to get Trish out of the yard and finish what he'd started. But for what? She had ruined the entire evening. Strangling her was no fun. This just wasn't right.

He pulled her by the arms and when he got to the car, he opened the trunk. He had to get rid of this mess, but he couldn't place her in there until her blood dried up. He didn't want to waste time trying to stop it on his own. He went inside, never mind being loud. He just didn't care. He stomped down the hall to the small guest bathroom, jerked the shower curtain down and raced back out.

He rolled Trish in the plastic sheeting and slung her into the trunk. He backed out of the driveway, spinning tires and burning rubber as he swayed back and forth on the pavement. He almost lost control, but managed to keep the car in the road. He raced through town, only thinking of the detrepanol he'd wasted, not to mention the wasted time he'd spent with Trish instead of Lori. What a mistake she had been.

Don't worry, Fredlee. It's okay. You can make up for it. Calm down before you send us both to the ER. Calm down and think.

He took a deep breath as he wound around tight curves and narrow streets. When he'd found a dark enough place, he slowed the car down, bringing it to a stop. He threw Trish into the ditch and never looked back.

His blood was boiling. He had to get Lori a friend, tonight. As he took in slow breaths, he saw two young girls on the sidewalk, walking slowly side by side and laughing.

Too young, Fredlee. Keep driving.

Soon, he saw a woman he hoped would do. She was walking along Tenth Street, swinging a beaded purse. Freddy knew there was a club just a block from here and assumed she was headed to her car after a night on the town.

He pulled up to her and leaned over to the passenger side window. He rolled it down and saw that she had stopped. Smiling, she leaned in to him.

"Hey, sugar. You looking for a date?"

"What?" Freddy was a little distraught and didn't realize that the woman was a prostitute.

"I said, are you looking for a date? Someone to give you some attention and make you feel good, baby?"

Freddy felt sick to his stomach. He didn't understand what women wanted, or men as far as that went. He couldn't fathom why anyone would want what *they* did.

Lori was all he needed and she was just the right temperature for him. Nothing alive could feel that sweet. He shook his head and heaved as he rolled the window up.

"Hey, you jerk! I was talking to you!" the woman shouted.

Freddy paid her no attention as he cruised on. When he saw the girl getting into a car just up ahead, he felt confident that she would suffice. He pulled the car up next to hers, got out of his car, and walked boldly up to her. She was just cranking up when she saw him approaching.

"Hi, ma'am. Could you help me, please? I'm not familiar with this area, and I'm lost. Could you tell me how to get back to, um, I think it's called Garris Street?"

Freddy knew full well there wasn't a Garris Street around here. He smiled down at the young girl and she was happy to help.

"I don't think there is a Garris Street. But there is a Green Street a few blocks back and a Gunther Avenue on the other side of town. I think that's the only G streets there are."

"How do I find Gunther? That may be it. I guess I forgot the street name."

The girl smiled a gorgeous smile and Freddy knew that this was right. When she started trying to tell him how to get to Gunther, he reached in, shot the detrepanol in her arm and smiled back at her.

"Don't worry. It won't hurt. But if you want to live, you need to step out of your car and walk calmly to mine." The girl opened her door, and watching Freddy the whole time, walked quietly with him. She sat down in the seat and started to feel the effects as the chemicals took control.

Freddy quickly hog tied the girl and pushed her across the back seat. She was begging and pleading, of course, saying things like, please don't hurt me, I'm too young to die. The usual crap he'd heard already.

He just wanted to get this done and take her to Lori. She was expecting a friend and he had promised.

It was getting late and Freddy had no time to waste. Carolyn would be up in less than four hours cooking breakfast for the two of them. He was exhausted, ill, and ready to end this. He stopped the car in the drive, got out and pulled her up to him. He untied her feet, leaving her hands strapped together.

"Let's make something clear, sweetie. I'm in charge, I'm really in a bad mood and if you give me a problem, you won't live to see the sunrise."

She shook her head, her eyes swollen from crying. Her head was spinning and she felt the effects of the drugs in her system full force. She wasn't sure what was happening, but she was sure that this man meant business. He wasn't a man, she noted. A teenager, maybe seventeen, eighteen at the most.

"Now walk."

Freddy led her into the building. He really would like to talk to her, get to know her. Maybe even ask her name, but time was of the essence. Inside, he gave her specific instructions.

"Get up on the table. I won't hurt you. I just need your help."

He untied her hands.

Hearing this, she felt a little more relaxed. He wasn't going to hurt her.

"Unzip your pants, but don't take them off. I only want to see your stomach."

She did as she was told.

"Good job. Now, I'm going to cut your hair."

He cut quickly, scraping and nicking her head and neck in several places. When that happened, she let out a little whimper, but remained still. She could see the determination in his eyes and decided to just do what she was told. This would be over soon and he would free her. He had told her that in those exact words. She never flinched as he shaved down the sprigs of black from her scalp. She didn't even try to escape when he held her ear up for her to see.

"Work of art. That's what you are, babe. A precious work of art. Good enough to hang in a museum."

The only time she tried to raise up, maybe escape, was when he jabbed her stomach with the needle. It plunged deeper than necessary, but that's what happens when plans are ruined.

Just don't get sloppy, Fredlee. Take your time. You know what you need. Go slow and do it right.

The machine switched on and as this stranger felt the formaldehyde enter her blood stream, she tried to scream. But the gag Freddy had used was too tight and she vomited in her mouth, gagging and choking.

Vomit rolled up her nasal passage and stung. The place where there was an ear a moment before was now pounding, her head throbbing, but none of that compared to the sheer anguish she felt in her veins. It only lasted for about ten seconds, maybe less.

I really need to time it, next time. Just for kicks. See how long they last. I might make a bet on duration, Freddy thought to himself.

When the woman quit moving and the blood was all gone from her, along with the contents from her stomach and other internal cavities, he unhooked her, quickly pulled Lori from her drawer and sat her up near the dead woman.

"Lori, look! I have you a friend," Freddy whispered.

"What's your name?" Lori asked.

Freddy wasn't sure what to say. He was so furious when he took her, he didn't know what her name was. He felt a rush of frustration as he stood, not knowing what he should say.

"I don't know, Lori. I'm so sorry. I never asked her what her name was."

"Then she won't work, will she, Fredlee?"

"I suppose not. I'll do better next time, I promise."

He carefully replaced Lori and slid the girl with no name in the drawer next to her. He really didn't even want her now. Not knowing her name had ruined the fun for him and Lori.

You are such a frickin screw up! But if you really don't want her, toss her in the attic, Fredlee. No one will ever find her and she'll be out of sight, out of mind. Lori will never know, will she? And I can tell you this. You never know when you'll be glad you have the wench. Trust me. Someday, you might just be glad to have her around.

Chapter Twelve

Detective Mark Leland walked around the area where Trish's body lay. He examined the street from one end to another.

"What did you see last?"

He was trying to get a feel for the situation, something he'd learned to do over the years. Sometimes, he could learn more about a crime by just assessing the area and the scene.

"You ready, sir?" the coroner asked.

Leland nodded his head as the coroner bagged and tagged the body of Trish Colbert. But he remained on the scene for some time.

It was obvious that Trish had been strangled, but there was more than that. She was missing her right ear. As he examined the side of her head, he could also tell that the cut was clean and precise. Whoever did this knew what he was doing.

There was a bloody purse tossed not far from where the body lay. Leland had carefully opened it and found twenty-three dollars bills, two quarters, a dime and three pennies. Her identification was still neatly tucked inside a small, pink wallet. "Whoever did this wasn't interested in money," the detective whispered as he bagged the contents of the purse in one clear bag, the purse itself in another.

Crime scene investigators had dusted the entire perimeter for prints, but nothing had turned up. All Leland could hope for was a clue on Trish's corpse. A fiber, a hair, anything that might bring her killer to justice.

As the coroner placed Trish's body into a body bag, Leland knelt down as close as he could without getting in the way. Her head had been freshly shaved. This was the work of someone with all the right tools to accomplish an exact mission, but would he ever figure it out? Thus far, the puzzle was missing too many pieces.

"Detective Leland?"

Leland looked up and saw Officer Brant standing beside him. He didn't know when he'd arrived or how long he'd been standing there.

"Yeah," Leland responded blandly.

"Another girl is missing. Her mom is at the station house now. A Rebecca Lewis."

Leland closed his eyes and drew in a breath. "Go on, tell me what she's saying."

Brant began by telling him that Mrs. Lewis was a wreck. "Rebecca was supposed to be home at eleven last night, but never showed."

Detective Leland stood and patted Brant on the back.

"I'll come back here later. I just know there's something I haven't seen that is staring me right in the face. And when I find it, I'll catch the bastard responsible."

Officer Brant shook his head in agreement before asking his next question.

"What about the crime scene tape? You want to leave it up for a day or two longer?"

"Most definitely. Keep it closed off as long as you can, Brant. Thanks."

Leland walked past reporters and onlookers as he climbed in his black and white. He made his way back to the station slowly. He really didn't want to talk to Mrs. Lewis now. He had to contact the Colbert family, a job he dreaded more than anything.

When he walked into the station, he nodded at several officers, busy doing the things that they were assigned to do. He noticed the graying lady sitting in a wooden chair almost immediately. She was sitting perfectly straight and both her feet were tapping in unison.

He could tell who she was. Parents of missing children were all the same. But this town was too small for this. Nothing like this ever happened in Wadesboro. But it *had happened* and he would see to it that justice was served.

"Mrs. Lewis?" he asked calmly.

"Yes, I'm Brenda Lewis. Have you found my daughter? I heard a body was located this morning. Is it my Becky?"

"Come this way, ma'am and we'll talk. Would you like some coffee?"

"Oh God! It is Becky. You found her body, didn't you?"

Leland stood by the coffee pot hoping she'd say yes and he'd pour them both a cup. But when she began to melt down, he aborted the idea and held her arm as he led her into his office.

"We did find a body. But I'm very doubtful that it's your daughter. Can you describe her for me?"

Brenda Lewis took a deep breath. "She has a mole on her left cheek. And her right ear has a scar from where she attempted to pierce it herself."

Well, that sure won't help, Detective Leland thought. "What else? How tall is your daughter? About how much would you say she weighs?"

As Brenda gave a complete detailed description of her daughter under teary eyes, Detective Leland took down notes. In his mind, he was sure this body wasn't Rebecca, but he couldn't tell her that until he knew for certain.

Right now, it was too hard to know for sure that this was actually Trish Colbert. The picture on her license was clear enough, but the body heading to the coroner's office wasn't as clean.

"We are investigating several missing persons reports and we are doing everything we can to find the person responsible. The coroner is working with this victim and as soon as I can tell you something, I'll call you."

He stood and offered Brenda a hand. She rose, nodded, and walked toward the door. Leland went back into his office and shut the door. He didn't see that Brenda never left. She sat in that same wooden chair all afternoon, waiting to hear if her daughter was alive or dead.

The detective had a mound of paperwork to do. He hated this part of the job. He really wanted to get back to where the woman had been located. He would, eventually. After four hours of filling in blanks and signing on dotted lines, he had waited as long as he cared to.

Leland picked up his phone and watched as the dial slowly turned and dropped back to its original position each time he turned the rotary. "Coroner's office," he heard on the other end.

"Yes, this is Detective Mark Leland from Anson County. How long till we know something about that body you collected this morning?"

"Actually, Detective, I was just about to call you. One female body, age nineteen, cause of death, asphyxia. Right now, that's all I can tell 'ya."

"That's all I needed for now. Thanks a bunch, Randy."

"My pleasure," the state coroner responded.

"At least I know it ain't Rebecca Lewis," Leland said aloud inside his office. He happened to glance out toward the chair Mrs. Lewis had taken earlier and was stunned to see her still sitting there. He looked up at the clock. That poor woman had sat there for four hours waiting to hear something.

He made his way back across the room and when she saw him, she stood, looking directly in to his eyes.

"Good news, Mrs. Lewis. The woman we found is not Rebecca."

Brenda grabbed her chest in relief. "How can you be sure?" she asked innocently.

"You said your daughter was seventeen, correct?"

The teary eyed woman nodded.

"The woman we discovered this morning was nineteen, confirmed by the coroner just now."

"But that means she's still out there. She could be cold, hungry—" Her voice dropped off.

"I can assure you, Mrs. Lewis, we are doing everything we can to locate your daughter and I will contact you as soon as I know anything concrete."

"Thank you, Detective," Brenda whispered.

As Brenda left the station, she couldn't help feeling relieved that her daughter wasn't on a coroner's table somewhere, but felt guilty for thinking that way, too. Because somewhere, someone was getting the news that their daughter was.

Chapter Thirteen

Freddy didn't sleep well that night. He had disappointed Lori. He had disappointed himself, too. He had to get things together and do this right.

He made sure Carolyn was sound asleep, and then dragged No Name, the girl he had killed in vain, up the stairs and pulled down the attic ladder. It squeaked loudly and he froze at the sound. It was so loud compared to the stillness of the house.

When Carolyn didn't wake, he pulled No Name up into the darkness of the attic and slid her across to the far corner. He took the time to wrap her body in plastic and taped it carefully around the seams. He wasn't sure that this would work, but for now it would surely do. Later, he may find a better way to store her corpse. He was so frustrated he didn't really care if the mice chewed her body completely away.

Two nights later, when Carolyn was in her own world, oblivious to Freddy, he carried Lori up stairs to his room. The night was perfect as the lovers made up.

"I'm so sorry, Freddy. I shouldn't have been so angry. You were so thoughtful to find me a friend and what do I do? I nagged you simply because I didn't know her name. Forgive me?"

"Of course I forgive you, baby. Can you forgive me?"

"For what? You didn't do anything wrong, my love."

"Yes, I did. I expected you to be happy with a complete stranger. That was careless of me. I was selfish to think you'd be happy that way."

Lori kissed Freddy slowly and passionately as he worked her hands up and down his sides. When they finished their love making, Freddy wrapped her arms around him and kissed her neck.

"Maybe next time, you can go with me. You should help me find someone to keep you company."

Lori was pleased and smiled the biggest smile she'd ever shown. "You mean it? I can go with?"

"I think you should."

As they slipped into sleep, Freddy smiled. His life was finally coming together and was proving to be full of promise.

* * * * * * *

Two months later, when he'd hoped the cops weren't quite as vigilant, and after Carolyn had made her way upstairs and snuggled under her blankets, Freddy dressed Lori in a gorgeous outfit he'd found in his mother's dresser.

"It's a little outdated, babe."

Lori didn't mind. She was very happy and eager to get going.

They drove into Albemarle, a town a little larger than Wadesboro. They had to be careful. Policemen were searching for Trish and No Name, and the Underhill family was relentless in their search to find Erin. As Freddy read about the disappearances in the local paper, he smiled. No one would ever suspect him and he was very careful to leave no clues behind.

According to *The Ansonian*, No Name was actually Rebecca Lewis, age seventeen. She had last been seen in Rockingham. Friends reported seeing her stop at the Fast Mart on Hwy. 74. The clerk inside remembered that she'd purchased gas and a pack of gum. He was sure she had left in her own car, or maybe it was a brown sedan. He had seen so many people that night, it was hard to tell.

No one had seen her after that, except for Freddy, of course. She was just in the wrong place at the wrong time and very convenient to take. The clerk was mistaken, but Freddy didn't care. Rebecca had left her car on the side of the road and was simply giving Freddy directions. It was that easy.

Her car would be located, several miles away and closer to Wadesboro, with no fingerprints or clues to help Leland.

Now, Freddy and Lori were slowly driving in downtown Albemarle, about thirty or so miles from the attention of the cops. They stopped at Pop's Drive-In for a shake and some fries and that's when they saw her. Freddy was pulling out again before he could even place an order with a carhop.

He had to be careful, Lori reminded him. When Lisa pulled out onto the main street, Freddy followed in behind her. At the light, she turned right. When she slowed down at the next street, it was perfect. The road was dark and lonely.

Freddy jumped out and ran to her car. "I'm sorry to bother you ma'am, but I'm very turned around. Could you help me a little?"

The lost ruse had worked before, so he was willing to try it once more.

Lisa rolled her window down just enough to hear him. "What do you need?" Lisa was a smart girl and knew not to ever get out of her car for a stranger, especially on a dimly lit side street.

"Actually, I'm trying to find Pop's Drive-In. I have a date there and I thought I knew where it was."

"Oh, that's an easy one. In fact, I just left from there."

"Groovy!" Freddy shouted.

As she began trying to give him directions, he acted more and more confused.

"Is that this street?" Freddy pointed behind him.

"No, that's Third Street. You need Pert Street."

"But where is that?"

Lisa took a deep breath and climbed from the safety of her car. She was turning around to point when she noticed Lori sitting in the passenger seat. She could tell that it was a woman, but the night was too dark to lend details to her badly decaying face.

"I thought you were on your way to a date?"

"I am, with you, darling."

Lisa was a handful. Freddy had an awful time convincing her to get in the Impala with him and Lori. For some reason, she was afraid of Lori in the beginning.

He had found, however, that letting Lori tag along was the best way to find a great friend for her. She was the one to spot Lisa and begged, yes, begged Freddy to pick her up. It took two complete vials of detrepanol to subdue her, but in the end, Lisa was perfect.

She had been very obliging after she was subdued. She had told them her name and everything else Freddy asked. She was terrified and was willing to do whatever it took to survive.

In the end, Lisa succumbed to the embalming process like all the others and looked so much better when it was all over. After the procedure, Freddy toted Lisa in right past his mother and up the stairs.

Carolyn sat in the den in front of the television. She heard a noise from the kitchen, but nothing registered for her. She couldn't seem to decipher one sound from another anymore. Even though she sat there in front of the set, she stared at it, wondering what they were saying and why it made no sense to her. When Freddy called out to her minutes later, she turned and smiled toward her son.

"Mom, it's time for bed. Come on and I'll help you get tucked in."

It was sad, really. For years, Carolyn had tucked her little boy in, kissed him goodnight, and turned out his lamp. Now, it was he doing the same for her.

She rose from the sofa and walked by Freddy and up the stairs. He followed behind her, curious to see what she would do. She went into the bathroom, shut and locked the door, and turned on the shower. Freddy heard the shrill sound coming from the faucet and knew immediately that she was showering.

For the last four months, he'd been the one to turn on the water and tell her it was time for a shower. He stood at the door, listening.

"Mom?"

But Carolyn didn't answer. He slid down the wall and waited for her to turn off the water. Twenty minutes later, it was still running and she still wasn't answering.

Freddy found a hairpin on her dresser and carefully unlocked the door. The steam from the hot water made the air thick and hard to breathe. Carolyn was crouched in the corner of the tub in a ball as the water poured down on her scalding her body.

Freddy quickly turned the knob to off and grabbed a towel from the closet. Covering his mother, he gently picked her up and sat her on the toilet. Her raw skin grew pinker as he assessed the damage. He knew right away that Carolyn was burned badly and in pain, yet she only smiled at him and drifted off again into her own private world.

Fredlee, don't you know what this means? Ever hear of a mercy killing? That's what you've got to do. Put her out of her misery. And when you do, you'll have the whole house to yourself. Imagine that! You and your pretties can have the pad to yourselves. Do it, Fredlee. Do it.

Freddy tried to drown out the voice. He couldn't say he *loved* his mother, but he did have a deep respect for the woman. He just couldn't fathom killing her.

He opened the medicine cabinet and began to fumble for ointment to cover her burns. When he'd found something, he knelt down to her. Carolyn grabbed his hand and pushed it away with the first touch.

"I know it hurts, mom. But I have to. If we don't take care of this, you could get very sick." When Carolyn spoke, it startled Freddy. She hadn't said anything coherent since Fred's funeral.

"I'm already sick, Freddy. You and I both know it."

Freddy didn't know how to respond to that. His inside-voice was ranting and raving about mercy killings, his mom was finally talking and suddenly, he heard Lori calling him from his room.

Carolyn turned her head and raised one eyebrow when Freddy's voice changed to accommodate Lori's voice.

"Freddy? What's wrong? When are you coming to bed, baby?" Freddy ignored Lori as he continued looking at his mom.

"Freddy? I'm lonely in here. Come to bed, darling." With that, Freddy just couldn't ignore her any longer. He was totally committed to Lori and wanted to please her in every way.

"Freddy? What are you doing? What's that you're saying?" Carolyn whispered.

"Mom, I'm going to give you something for pain. It will make you sleepy, but you need to rest now."

Carolyn nodded as Freddy reached for her migraine pills. He poured the entire bottle into his hand and counted thirty-two pills. That was enough. Carolyn swallowed them down obediently. Freddy sat by his mother, holding her hands. She looked to him and as she became very drowsy, she said something that would haunt him for the rest of his life.

"I forgive you, son. I forgive you for killing your father and me."

Then she slumped over the toilet and her head would have hit the hard tile if Freddy hadn't been expecting it. He caught her as she fell and he toted her to bed and covered her up.

He stood watching her die until Lori called out to him again. "Baby, I want you so bad. Come make me happy. Please?"

How could he say no to the one woman that would never leave him? It wasn't possible. So he turned to leave Carolyn's room.

"Good night, mom. Sleep tight."

He clicked off the light and headed to his room. His inside-voice was right again. He now had the whole house to himself. He and his treasures could do whatever, whenever.

Because he had not yet attended college, let alone received a degree, he couldn't perform the services for his mother. He called on Hampton Thomas again, as he had for his father. Carolyn lay in state in the front room for two days and was buried in the family cemetery behind their home. The infants that had preceded her in death lay to the left of her and Fred to her right.

Freddy tried desperately to feel something for the loss of his mother, but Lori kept him strong and his inside voice continued to come and go. He kept himself busy preparing for school. He and Lori both agreed on morning classes. He would come home tired, but he would come home each night. And as long as he knew Lori would be waiting for him, he was willing to drive the long route each evening.

When August finally arrived, he was all set to go. Lori assured him she and Lisa would be fine during the day. Freddy placed the two of them in the living room, turned on the television, and kissed his wonderful loves goodbye.

College was very predictable. Most of the things he heard during the day were things he already knew. His father had taught him well. School was going to be a breeze.

Other students were excited about ball games and parties. All Freddy could do was count down the hours until he was finally home with Lori.

He didn't worry about the same things in college that had occupied his mind in high school. Even though he had trouble focusing during the day, his inside-voice remained quiet, for the most part. The students were more mature and never bothered him. That in itself was a relief.

Every evening when his final class was over, he raced to his car and sped home as quickly as he could to be with the woman of his dreams. And every night, he would find her waiting patiently for him.

They would sometimes talk for hours about their day, while other times, they were too busy with touching and kissing and loving each other to talk.

Chapter Fourteen

When Freddy saw just how happy Lori was with Lisa, he surprised her one night by bringing home Paula. Lori was ecstatic to get to go into the building to watch as Freddy prepared the sweet young girl. In the end, Paula looked so much like Lori. Paula was glad, too. She told Freddy and Lori just how happy he'd made her.

Then Christmas came, and as a special gift for Lori, he brought home Michelle. Michelle proved to be an even greater challenge. Police were on the lookout for a kidnapper. He was supposedly driving a tan or brown sedan, but there were only two witnesses and one of them was high on acid and couldn't be considered reliable. The other was the clerk at the Fast Mart and he didn't really know anything.

Freddy had gone all the way to Charlotte that night by himself. It wouldn't have been a surprise if Lori had known. He wrapped around the mall two, three, four times before eying her. She had been shopping and was loaded down with packages. She lugged two large bags as well. Freddy stopped the car and walked right up to her.

"Oh, my! You need a little help, don't you?" His smile was sincere and Michelle had no reason not to trust the sweet young boy.

"Sure! Thank you!" Michelle accepted his help right away. "My car is all the way over there." She nodded in the opposite direction of the Impala.

"Well how about this. My car is right here. I'll drive you over."

"I couldn't let you do that. That's too much." Michelle really wanted to take him up on his offer, but that seemed to be asking an awful lot of a stranger.

"It's no trouble, really. In fact, it would help me earn a new badge in Y.B.B." Y.B.B., or Young Baptist Boys, was a well-known organization at the time within the Bible Belt of the nation.

"Are you sure?"

"Yes, ma'am. Here, I'll get the door for you."

He held the door for Michelle and as she was fumbling with her bags and boxes, he injected her with a good healthy dose of the *sleepy stuff,* as Lori liked to call it. Just like all the others, Michelle had winced, shot him a terrified look of shock and slowly relaxed down onto the vinyl.

That night, Freddy took as many back roads as he could to get Michelle home safely. Cops were swarming the place and plenty were just looking to fill a holiday quota. Michelle stirred a little, but the increased dosage of detrepanol had really been an excellent improvement. Freddy was becoming an old pro at abduction.

Freddy's mind raced about as he drove the long way home with Michelle slumped over beside him. He thought about the things his dad had said to him and the bragging his mom had always done. Freddy *was* good. Good at everything he did. The only mistake he'd made was the night Trish had fought him. She had been a very detrimental part of his plan.

He carried Michelle in, wrapped tightly in his arms and bound and gagged. She looked around momentarily, and then collapsed again. The only part about the increased dosage was that Lori's friends weren't completely aware of what was happening as he worked.

He really liked talking to them and telling them what was happening. He enjoyed watching the fear dance around in their dilated pupils. Lori would be so angry if she knew that, so he kept that little tidbit to himself.

He lay Michelle on the worktable and placed a small bottle of smelling salts underneath her nostrils. "Wake up, sweetie! We're home!" he crooned.

Michelle looked around, confusion taking over. She wanted to tell him she wasn't home. She wanted to tell him her family would be looking for her. She tried to speak through the gag, but it was too tight around her mouth. She wanted to kick, scream, scratch, bite, whatever she could to get away, but she lay there helpless under the influence of the drugs and confinement.

Freddy rummaged through her purse until he found what he needed.

"Your name is Michelle?"

She nodded.

"And that's what your friends call you?"

Again, Michelle agreed.

"That's great. Lori would want to know. Lori is my girlfriend and she loves having company. So I thought you'd make a great present for her. Isn't that exciting? You're going to love her. She is so sweet and tender."

Freddy continued to brag on his Lori as Michelle began to cry. She wasn't sure what was happening right away.

"I know you want to meet her and she will be ecstatic to meet you. But, first things first."

Freddy began to cut then shave Michelle's long, dark ringlets away. He stroked her head, her face and held her head tightly in his hands as he cut away her ear. Michelle was trying to figure out what the small piece of skin was that he held in front of her.

"It's just that Lori doesn't have an ear or hair. So, to make her feel better about things, I always do this first. But don't worry. The others look just like you will."

As he inserted the embalming needle, Michelle started to put two and two together.

This isn't happening. It can't be happening. Not to me. Not me.

Those were the last thoughts to race through Michelle's mind. The pain that followed proved too much and her body gave way to shock.

Chapter Fifteen

Time was speeding by for Freddy. The only time it seemed to stand still was when he was at school, away from Lori. Christmas came and went and finally, spring break arrived. He had planned to stay very busy those two weeks.

He sat at the kitchen table with Lori to his right and Lisa to his left. Michelle was in the den enjoying a very good novel that Freddy had placed in her hands. It was some romance novel he'd found when going through his mother's things.

When he opened the morning paper, the headlines immediately caught his attention.

Real Life Horror Story Stuns County

On the morning of June 7, the body of a young woman was found just outside of town, near Morven. The body was confirmed to be that of Trish Colbert, from Scotland County. Colbert was reported missing on the evening of Friday, October 6 when she didn't return home from a trip to the Anson County Library. Librarians recall seeing her leave the building, but no one saw her after that. Her Volkswagen Beetle was discovered in the parking lot where she had parked it that morning. According to the state coroner, her death was ruled homicide by strangulation. Police Detective Mark Leland made the following statement to our reporter:

"We are now working in collaboration with the Charlotte- Mecklenburg Police Department concerning a young woman reported missing from Eastland Mall in Charlotte. Michelle Carthage, 19, was last seen as she was leaving the mall on the evening of Friday, December 20.

"At this time, we cannot determine if the two missing women are in any way connected."

Even though Detective Leland says the two are more than likely coincidence, it is better to be safe than sorry. We encourage you to stay away from isolated areas, walk in groups, and don't talk to anyone you are not completely acquainted with.

"Anyone with information regarding the whereabouts of Michelle Carthage is asked to contact your local police immediately. The Carthage family is offering a reward for any information that leads to Miss Carthage's safe return."

According to our sources, even though it has not been made official by officers, there are three other open missing persons reports from Stanly, Richmond, and Anson Counties.

More information will be given as it becomes available to us.

Freddy read the article and looked over the top edge of the paper to see Lori staring at him.

"I'm worried, Freddy. What if—"

"What if what, Lori? Haven't I taken very good care of you? I'm smart, yes? I know what I'm doing. No one will ever suspect me or think for a moment that I could have anything to do with, with —" Freddy tossed the paper up and slowly each section floated down around him. "With any of this."

He rose from the table and headed into the den where Michelle sat patiently waiting. He smiled down at her and gently pulled her up to him.

"I think it's time for someone to get dressed. I have a gift for you, Michelle."

Michelle squealed with delight. "What is it, baby? What do you have for me?"

Freddy toted her body up the stairs and opened his bedroom door. He slid her down on the floor in front of his bed.

"Wait right here, beautiful you."

When Freddy had Lori, Michelle, Paula, and Lisa all lined up on the floor in front of his bed, he began.

"As you know, I've taken great pains to bring you all here to live with me. I've sacrificed a great deal to make this happen. Don't get me wrong, I've loved every minute of it."

He paced the floor as the girls watched him.

"Thank you, baby," Lori whispered.

Freddy knelt down to her. "Thank you, Lori. For being so grateful." As he kissed her, he placed her boney hands on his chest and began to stroke himself.

He cradled her head in his hands and continued. "I think that in order for you to really understand what I go through to bring you here, it's time you watch what I do."

Michelle gasped. "You mean it? We get to watch you work?"

He knew they'd be thrilled. He smiled in delight as each doll in his pretty collection giggled, making sounds that would cause any man to feel week in the knees.

Freddy took a box from his closet shelf and set it on Michelle's lap. "Open it."

He had to help Michelle, but with his hands on top of hers, he pulled a yellow ribbon and the pretty bow began to untangle.

Then the two of them took the top off, revealing a bright orange sheaf dress with pink trim. Michelle once again yelped in surprise at the gorgeous dress.

"Don't be jealous, ladies. I have something new for all of you."

Lori laughed as he placed a wrapped box on her lap. She received a green dress with a floral print.

"Just like I had before. Oh, Freddy, I love it. Thank you so much!"

"You deserve it, Lori. I love you. I love you like I've never loved and never thought possible. When I'm with you, I feel something, a good warm feeling."

Lori continued to smile at Freddy as Paula and Lisa opened their gifts. The surprise in Paula's box revealed a big, blue bow in the center of a blue and white gingham mini dress. Lisa had one similar, only it was pink and white. They all loved their new dresses and told Freddy so.

"Now, later on, when it's a little safer to hunt, I'll go find you a perfect girl to spend time with. It's kind of groovy, don't you think? Having so many wonderful friends? A lady for each room in the house. That's my goal. I've got to do something with those dreadful front rooms, though."

Freddy was lost in thought as he dressed each body. He had given those rooms a lot of consideration lately. He knew he needed the parlor to renew the practice after graduation. It's just that he'd always hated the drab colors and dark patterns. It was too solemn.

"You know, Freddy. You could just paint the walls to a lighter, fresher color. Maybe change the drapes and get the furniture upholstered in a spring shade."

Lori always made so much sense. She always made him think clearly.

"Groovy idea! That's what we'll do, if I ever graduate." Freddy rolled his eyes as he spoke.

"Oh, you know you will. I know it's hard to leave me every day, but I promise, it's for the best." Lori ran her fingers through Freddy's hair as she spoke softly in his ear. The act got Freddy aroused and as the two made love, the other girls watched on.

"Maybe someday, you'll think about sharing our love," Freddy teased Lori.

"Actually, we do have enough to share."

Freddy rose up on his elbows and thought about that idea. He flopped down hard on his back. "Where have you been all my life, sweetheart?"

"I've been waiting for you, Freddy."

* * * * * * * *

That night, when darkness fell and Freddy felt safe to do so, he helped Lori out to the building.

Lori was so excited. She couldn't believe that he was allowing her this opportunity again.

After he had Paula, Michelle, and Lisa in place, he promised to be home soon with a beautiful new girl for them to enjoy. He turned back to face his lovely girls and saw Michelle wink at him. He turned to Lori and noticed that Lori was looking away, so he winked back.

"Be back soon, girls. Be good!" he yelled over his shoulder as he locked the door.

Amber was standing at the bus stop. Her hands quivered under the foggy night air. Freddy had planned to go into another town to shop, and when he saw her, he was very pleased that he'd gone so far from home. The three-hour trip to Raleigh was sure to be worth it.

Amber's brown hair was cut short and bounced around as she turned from side to side. No doubt now, women were looking at every corner for a murderer and kidnapper, even this far from home. That made Freddy a little proud and very conscientious.

Freddy parked the car a block away. He casually strolled up to Amber and pushed his hands in his pockets. "Cold tonight, huh?"

Amber looked straight ahead and barely nodded. "Sure is."

"How much longer before the bus stops?"

"It's usually a little late on Friday nights. It should be here in less than fifteen minutes."

"That's good. I don't really feel safe with that freak on the loose. Have you read about the kidnappings in the paper?"

Amber turned to face him. "I don't understand how girls can go missing like that without a clue."

"It's crazy. I just hope they find him soon."

"You and me both," Amber agreed.

Freddy held out a hand. "Freddy Lee."

Amber hesitated briefly, then obliged. "Amber Hilliard."

The two shook hands and Freddy smiled innocently. "You know, you really shouldn't be out alone now."

"Night classes. I don't have much choice."

"Oh, I see. Night classes for what?"

"Nursing school. Two semester to go!" Amber gave a thumbs up as she talked.

"Congratulations, Amber. That's great. I'm close to graduating myself."

"Oh, yeah? What's your major?"

"You'll laugh. You'll say how gross it sounds."

"No, I won't. Really. What do you do?"

"I'm a mortician."

"Eww...that's gross!" Amber laughed. "Just joking. Actually, I think that's kind of cool," she said.

"It's all I've ever done. My dad taught me and his dad taught him. Not too bad, once you get used to it."

Amber shook her head in agreement. "My mom is a nurse and her mom is, too. I guess old habits die hard, or something like that."

"Guess so."

"So what brings you out on a night like this, anyway?" Amber asked, trying to remain cautious but friendly.

Freddy had no cue cards. He was finding this relaxing and natural. "Just headed home. My car stalled out."

"Oh, that's too bad."

"Actually, Amber, I think if I had a little help, I could get it going. I don't suppose you'd feel comfortable helping me, would you? I could give you a ride home after."

Amber thought for a moment, then replied, "Sure, I guess I could. But I'll warn you. I know nothing about cars."

"It's okay, I just need someone to turn the key while I tinker under the hood a little." As they walked along, Freddy scanned the area. No one around, no one to see.

"Well, that I can do."

"It's just right over there." Freddy pointed to his Impala, which was beginning to look a little old, now. "I guess I should go ahead and just get a new one, but if I can get this one to work, I'll save the money, you know?"

"Oh, I agree. I hope to have a car soon, too. But for now, I'll take the bus and save my money."

When they reached the car, Freddy felt around in his pocket until he had the syringe ready. He removed the safety cap and as Amber turned to him for instructions, he jabbed her neck with the needle. She went down faster than the others, probably because she'd been at school all day and was exhausted.

"I think you need a nap, Amber."

Amber didn't come to until they were home and she was on the worktable, tied down with leather belts. One strapped across her chest, the other at her hips. She was seeing double and nothing made sense.

"She's awake, Freddy! She's finally awake!" Amber heard a female voice in the distance say.

She strained her neck to see the woman who was talking, but saw four women. She couldn't tell which one had spoken. Her blurry vision was slowly starting to improve as Freddy leaned in over her.

"Well, it's about time, Amber! Welcome home. This is Lori, my girlfriend. These are her friends."

As he named them all, he pointed at them and in a different voice for each one, told her hello.

When Amber could see clearly, fear filled her. Lori sat in a chair near her. Her blank, white eyes stared off into nothingness. The bald head and missing ear made her look as if she had been put through a blender.

"Don't be afraid, girlie," Freddy spoke for Lori. "This is a wonderful home and Freddy will take care of you, just as he does for us."

Amber looked behind Lori and saw Lisa, who was as disfigured as Lori was. She began to jerk, trying to free herself from the bands that held her tightly. Michelle and Paula sat near Lori, all the same distant look in their nonexistent eyes.

"Don't fight it, Amber," Freddy advised in his own voice. "You see, Lori and I are in love, but she gets lonely. She needs company while I'm at school. And when my parents were living here, she had to stay locked away in my room all day, every day. She was bored and lonely. So I found Paula, Lisa, and Michelle. They are so very happy here with me and you will be, too."

"I don't understand, Freddy." Amber tried to say.

Freddy held his head back and laughed loudly. The laughter echoed through the building and caused goose bumps to crawl down Amber's back. "I killed Trish Colbert. She got away from me and I had to kill her. It was a shame, too. She was going to be a work of art. Art imitating life! Ha! Get it?"

He made Lori laugh a little as he continued. "I dumped her. She ruined it for me. She ruined a great moment and I hated her for it."

Amber looked around desperately searching for a way out. Her restraints were too tight and she began pulling with all her might. The sound caught Freddy off guard.

"No! No! You are staying, Amber! I won't let another one escape. I'm in control. And you're becoming a part of my collection, Amber. It's your turn to become a work of art."

Amber didn't have time to respond. Freddy placed the needle under the skin on her stomach and flipped the machine on. He'd shave her bald and remove her ear later. Time was running out for Freddy. He felt the control slipping through his fingers and that was something he couldn't afford to lose.

He felt the anticipation as he watched the life slowly drain out of Amber. Two hours later, Amber was empty of her own fluids and filled with chemicals that would preserve her as they had the others.

Freddy was a little disappointed that Amber didn't fight harder than she did. She didn't spasm and writhe. It was a letdown. Freddy walked to Lori and pressed his lips to hers.

As they kissed, he began to slowly remove her pretty new dress. He pushed inside her harder than ever. This was different, but he liked it. He liked the harshness and so did Lori. As he made his way across the room to Michelle, he entered her with the same fierceness. Michelle moaned loudly as he continued.

Before they left the building, he had a turn with Lisa and Paula, too. Lori was right. The love they shared was too big not to incorporate the others.

He toted them each back into the house, Amber last. He had to unstrap her and dress her with the clothes he'd already purchased. They weren't a perfect fit, but close enough. After he'd shaved her head and took away the ear, she was as pretty as his other girls.

* * * * * * * *

Freddy sat in the living room, Lori by his side. Amber had been placed in the den, in front of the T.V. watching *Chico And The Man.* Michelle was upstairs, taking a nap. Freddy put Paula in the kitchen. She sat very naturally at the table, a cup of coffee and the *Ansonian* spilled out in front of her.

Freddy read from Michael Crichton's *Eaters of The Dead.* Lori had finished it last week and highly recommended it.

Freddy looked up briefly to find Lori gazing at him. She smiled, or Freddy imagined her smiling, and he rose up to softly kiss her sweet lips. The moment was spontaneous, and Lori loved that.

She loved that she was free now to roam the house, going wherever she pleased. She was sad that Carolyn was gone, and Fred, too. But now she and her friends could really feel at home.

It made her very happy the way Freddy carried her from room to room, getting lots of afternoon sunshine in the sunroom, sipping hot coffee in the kitchen, even bathing when Freddy felt she'd enjoy a nice, hot bath. It was wonderful having this freedom and no worries.

Chapter Sixteen

Detective Mark Leland was at a complete loss. He had called a meeting with other investigators from surrounding counties. As the men all took their seats around a large oak table, he began.

"Good morning. Thank you all for coming."

He walked to a board standing at the front of the room and flipped it over, revealing notes, newspaper clippings, and pictures of the women they had all been searching for. Some pictures were in black and white, while others were in full color.

"Here's what we know. In two years, six young women have gone missing, one turning up dead. On August first, 1973, Erin Underhill went skating with her cousin and a few friends. She was visiting her cousin on the night she went missing. They all say the same thing. Erin forgot her purse and went back out to the parking lot to get it. She never returned. No one saw a damn thing."

He was pointing to a picture of Erin as he spoke. The picture showed a lovely girl with long, red hair. She was smiling brightly.

"On Friday June 7, 1974, the body of Trish Colbert was found in a ditch in Morven. Her Volkswagen was still parked in the parking lot of the Anson County Library. When she was discovered, she was missing her right ear and had been shaved.

Cause of death was strangulation. Again, no one saw anything. Hell, it might not have a thing to do with Erin Underhill or the others. But why rule it out? Any suggestions?"

Leland stood still and waited. When no one said anything, he continued.

"Saturday, June 8, 1974, Rebecca Lewis was reported missing when she didn't return home from work that Friday evening. Again, no one saw a thing." As he pointed to a black and white portrait of Rebecca, he jotted down the name *Becky* underneath her smiling face.

"She too was from right here in Anson County."

"August 10, 1974, Lisa Poplin was last seen at Pop's Drive-In in Albemarle. She stopped on her way home from her grandmother's house for a milkshake and never made it home."

"October 15, 1974, Paula Herst of Monroe was waiting for her daughter to finish a piano lesson. She was last seen dropping her daughter off at a Mrs. Keller's Music Center. Her eleven-year-old daughter said she kissed her goodbye and told her she'd be back in an hour. She was going to drop off some dry cleaning while the child practiced piano. She never made it to the dry cleaners. Her car was parked on a side road three blocks from Keller's. The clothes she was supposed to take to be cleaned were still in the car. No hairs, no fibers from transfer, no prints, no nothing."

"Michelle Carthage, age nineteen, went Christmas shopping at Eastland Mall in Charlotte. It was the mall's grand opening and several storeowners and clerks saw her. They remembered that she was a big spender. She was last seen leaving Belk Department Store. That was on December 20, 1974."

Every officer and detective in the room looked at her picture. She was a stunning young woman and it was hard for them to move on when Leland continued.

"And that brings us to Amber Hilliard. Amber was a nursing student at Wake Tech. Her last class of the evening ending at seven P.M. her instructor talks very highly of her. She is a smart girl. Her roommate also says that she wasn't one to leave with someone she didn't know. If she was abducted, it was under duress, not willing." Leland tapped the board and stared out at the room full of men.

"Are they related?" Leland asked and waited for an answer.

"Come on, ladies. There has to be a common thread. Please, help me find it. What are we missing?"

Detective Landers, from Stanly County spoke up. "Could he be a doctor?"

Every one turned to face him and waited for an explanation.

"Trish Colbert had been disfigured. From the photos you have pasted up there, it looks to me like a clean, precise cut. Whoever did this must have a means to do so. Could any 'ole razor from any 'ole five and dime do that?"

Leland nodded. "He could be a doctor. Or at least have some workable knowledge of medical science."

"If Colbert is even related to the others," retorted Officer Kent, from Union County.

That comment caused a little hum to fill the room. Leland knew Kent was right. It was possible that Colbert wasn't even involved with the other cases.

It was then that Celeste Bringham began flipping through her own notes. Leland saw the stenographer unfolding notes and smoothing them out. He could tell by her expression that she had a bright bulb burning in her brain.

"Miss Celeste, is there something you'd like to add?" Celeste looked up, startled. Most of the men in the room chuckled amongst themselves at the idea that she could help with the case. Her job was to sit quietly and take notes.

"Actually, yes, sir, I do. I'm looking at the dates you've got highlighted on the board. These women were around the same age, but nothing more. No obvious links to put them together. And it may not mean a thing, but if you'll look back at the calendar, the days they were reported missing is the same. They were all abducted or reported missing on Fridays. Every one of them. I can't help but think your culprit does his work on Friday nights."

The room grew quiet as the policemen all started pulling out pocket calendars or flipping back through their own notes. Leland smiled. Finally, a common thread.

"Miss Celeste has a good point and it's not something that any of us saw before. Great job, Celeste. Maybe you should consider the police academy yourself."

No other cop seemed to agree with Detective Leland, but he was right. She had seen something that none of the cops had. She smiled and felt proud of her revelation, even if half the room *had* snickered at the thought of there ever being a female officer.

"As of right now, every county surrounding us should consider a Friday night curfew. It might make a few folks angry, but I'd rather have some pissed off kids and employers than another missing girl. All agreed?"

When everyone had either nodded or said "agreed", Leland made it clear that there would be an announcement made at all local high schools, community colleges, and news stations.

"We'll offer an official statement to the newspapers, too. And let's hope and pray this puts a real kink in this SOB's plans."

As the room cleared out, everyone was talking and whispering about the possibilities of these women all being taken by the same person, and possibly someone with a knowledge of medical procedure.

Celeste went back to her desk to transcribe all of her notes. As she walked out of the room, Leland once again thanked her.

"I may be very wrong. It could just be a coincidence." She shrugged her shoulders as she humbly looked down at her work.

"I don't know either, Celeste, but that idea you had could save another woman from being kidnapped."

She hoped he was right.

Chapter Seventeen

Freddy and Lori sat snuggled together on the sofa in the den. Freddy had placed Paula and Michelle in the sunroom. The girls always loved to sit out there together.

Sometimes, he placed them all together out there to soak in the warm afternoon sun. Today, only these two girls enjoyed it. Lisa was already in bed. She had told him just how tired she was, so Freddy tucked her in early. Amber was in the kitchen, enjoying a nice cup of hot chocolate.

In his mind, these corpses really did speak to him and they even ate and drank whatever he provided. It was no shock to him when they sometimes even complained. Most of the time, they all got along great, but there were moments when they bickered in Freddy's warped imagination.

This had been one of those occasions. Lisa and Lori had argued over the television and finally, Lisa told her to forget it. She had a splitting headache and was ready to rest. Toting her upstairs, Freddy had reprimanded her for her outburst. When she apologized to him and Lori, everything was back to normal.

The lovebirds were watching *Happy Days,* but mostly they kissed and held each other tightly. It was so nice to have a weekend home with no work scheduled for the following week. And as long as there were no deaths in the community, Freddy could relax for a change.

It seemed that the whole county celebrated with Freddy when he finally graduated. Everyone missed the quality of care and dignity offered by a family owned and operated business. When it came to work, Freddy was very professional. Everyone appreciated that. Fred Senior had taught him so many things that aren't learned in school and for that, Freddy was grateful.

As they were entangled in a passionate knot, a beeping sound blared from the set. The sound drew Freddy from his lover. The television screen went blue, then a symbol, an eagle, from the local station, WQRZ, filled the screen. Moments later, the camera showed Lauren Lane, the local newscaster, centered behind a desk.

"We're sorry to interrupt your television viewing, but Detective Mark Leland with the Anson County Sheriff's Department has issued the following statement:

"In light of the sudden disappearances of six local women and a seventh found dead, the Anson County Sheriff's Department has declared a curfew for all teens and young adults, ages fifteen to twenty-five. You should use caution at all times and arrive home no later than nine P.M. All employers are expected to respect this call as there are many employees that are in this age group. It is of utmost importance that you abide by this local law at all times, especially on Friday nights."

"According to Leland, all women abducted were reported missing either on Friday nights, or Saturday mornings. There is still no definite connection to the murder of Trish Colbert, but local and county officials are now in collaboration with surrounding counties to find and prosecute the person or persons responsible for these kidnappings, along with the death of Miss

Colbert. We will bring more to you as we are informed. Now, we take you back to your regularly scheduled programming."

As the screen went dark and then back to *Happy Days,* there was a still shot of The Fonz and Potsie in the Cunningham's living room. After several seconds, the sound continued, first with Fonzy saying *heeey,* then the audience laughing. After another few seconds, the actors began moving again and all was well in the homes of thousands of viewers.

Freddy wasn't as happy as all the other viewers tuning in. He rose from the sofa and felt the room spinning.

You idiot! What the hell is wrong with you? I've said it before and I'll say it again. You are a good for nothing loser who can't do a damn thing right. Not one thing.

"Freddy? What's the matter, baby?" Lori whined.

Freddy was having trouble focusing. His inside-voice was in stereo and Lori's voice was blasting at top volume.

He never spoke, simply stood and turned to face Lori. He shook his head in disbelief.

"What's *wrong*? How could you not see that there is a problem here?"

He was yelling loudly to drown out the voice in his head. Lori began to cry.

"Freddy! Calm down. Think about it. They said Friday nights, not *you.* They don't know who is responsible. They have no clue. Just start hunting on another day, that's all."

Lori's voice became calming and soothing to Freddy. She was right. They had nothing but dates.

"You always know just what to say, my princess. I love you for that. Thank you."

Freddy slid his arms around Erin Underhill's corpse and pulled her arms around his waist.

"I love you, too, baby. I love you more and more every day."

The night couldn't have ended up better. Freddy toted Lori upstairs and gently slid her under the covers. As he mounted over her, he softly kissed her forehead, then her cheek. Tenderly, he began to make Lori moan with pleasure. When he turned out the lamp, she was still moaning in satisfaction.

"I'm so lucky to have you, Lori."

"And so am I to have you, Freddy."

And they fell asleep in each other's arms.

Chapter Eighteen

1976

Detective Leland stared at the same board he'd prepared a year before. There had been no new clues and no leads at all. He had never felt so down. The Colbert family had stopped calling twice a day. At first, they began to only call once a day. Now, they were only calling a few times a week, at best.

Mrs. Brenda Lewis had a heart attack just before Christmas and died on Christmas day. She died never knowing the whereabouts of her daughter. Rebecca's father, Ron, had stopped by a few times, but seemed to give up hope of ever finding his daughter.

There were other families that called and came, hoping for information concerning their loved ones, but he had nothing to give him. He would always apologize and feel totally helpless.

Celeste Bringham knocked on Leland's door, bringing him back to reality.

"Come in, Celeste."

She entered his office and sat down opposite him.

"What's on your mind, Celeste?"

"I've been thinking."

Those were welcoming words to Mark Leland.

"There haven't been any new missing persons. That could mean one of a few things."

"Okay, go on," he said, as he knew something was brewing in that sharp mind of hers.

"First, we can hope the person responsible is dead. Only that would mean no closure to those affected. Second, maybe the curfew you had in place spooked him and he's just waiting for you to let your guard down. Another possibility is that he's taking girls that wouldn't be noticed or reported missing."

"No offense, Celeste, but I've thought of all those possibilities. In fact, I've thought of nothing else."

"Yes, sir. I understand that. But what if, well, what if you drew him out of hiding?"

"Go on, I'm listening.""

"If you announced that the perp had been arrested or even a new body reported missing, it could cause a reaction. If you're watching and waiting, you just might find him."

Leland sat quietly listening. "I'll take that in to consideration, Celeste. Thanks."

Celeste nodded and walked back toward the door. She paused for a moment before saying, "It's just that, well, those girls are about the age of my own daughter and I really want to see him caught."

"You and me both, Celeste."

Only an hour had passed when Leland had made a decision. He would offer a new report and hope Celeste was right. He called for her to come back into his office and together, she and the detective wrote an official statement for the newspaper.

On the evening of November14, Detective Mark Leland made the following statement on behalf of the Anson County Sheriff's Department:

"We have been investigating another kidnapping case. We believe the perpetrator is responsible for at least four other open missing persons cases ranging from 1973 to the present. The body of an unidentified woman was found on March 12 and in investigating that case, the Sheriff's department has made an arrest. The person brought in for questioning is being held without bond. We are asking that you continue to be vigilant and keep abiding by the nine o'clock curfew until further notice as we wait to confirm the identity of the victim.

The notice would be placed in tomorrow's *Ansonian*. They could only hope for the best. Leland contacted every detective in every county surrounding Anson in hopes that they would add more officers to the streets.

"If he reads this, he may just get angry that someone else is getting credit for his handiwork," Leland explained as he made his numerous calls.

* * * * * * * *

Now Leland needed to keep watch on the town throughout the weekend. Every available cop was cruising all over town. Undercover officers were placed in areas known to attract teens. There was one stationed at Roller Rinker's, McDonald's, and the downtown shopping strip.

When one policeman was too tired or needed a break, another one relieved him. In every town within a two hundred mile radius, officers were keeping close watch on their small populations. People seemed to feel the tension and whispered among themselves every time a cop was spotted.

We're being too obvious, Detective Leland thought. *If only we had more undercover officers to do the job. If only I had a five hundred officer task force.*

There were only eleven officers in the Anson County Sheriff's Department and at times, that seemed too many. Wadesboro wasn't a large town, but the bigger cities, like Monroe and Charlotte did have the manpower.

Hopefully, if the perp struck, it would be in a town with eyes and ears. Unfortunately, the kidnapper was keeping a quiet profile that weekend.

Freddy opened the morning paper as the girls all slept in. The false report was on the front page under the heading *Kidnapper Caught!* Freddy was enthralled by the statement. He read the article twice, then gingerly tossed the paper in the garbage.

Well, well, well, Freddy. Looks like you're off the hook. Time to get busy, wouldn't you say?

Freddy smiled. Yes, it was finally safe to hunt again. But he would have to be very careful. No slip ups, no escapes, no messes. And no witnesses.

He hurried upstairs, woke the girls, and called for a celebration.

"This is great, Freddy! Now we can finally bring another sister home!"

Lori had begun calling Paula, Michelle, Amber, and Lisa her sisters. Freddy loved that. It made him very happy to have such a large family. He'd always wanted that.

Freddy swung Lori around and around until they were both dizzy and laughing carelessly. Freddy lost balance and he and Lori both fell over and hit the floor. They were still laughing when Freddy cradled Lori's face in his hands and stared deep into her eyes.

Erin's eyes saw nothing. They were actually solid white. But Freddy looked to her and saw that she was staring right back at him. Her brown eyes were sparkling with the morning sun shining through a small slit in the shades.

"You are so beautiful, Lori."

He kissed her softly as Michelle, Paula, Lisa and Amber looked on. Freddy heard them whispering about how jealous they were of Lori. She had Freddy all to herself, except on occasion when they were feeling very giddy. Lucky for them, Freddy was feeling very giddy now and enjoyed all of his girls that morning.

"Freddy, you are the man!" Michelle hummed.

Freddy smiled down at her. He thought so, too. He had changed quite a bit over the years and the scrawny, geeky teenager was gone. His inside-voice had even noticed the change and no longer called him Fredlee. He was Freddy now, to everyone who really knew him.

* * * * * * * *

Detective Leland had smashed his fist into the metal locker in the changing room of the Sheriff's Department. He knew the Sheriff would be coming today and would give him a piece of his mind. For three days, every officer in the county had worked overtime.

"Do you know how much this is costing the county, Leland? Well, do you?"

Leland closed his eyes as he imagined what would be thrown his way.

Mark Leland was as helpless and clueless today as he was in 1973 when Erin Underhill first went missing. He had exhausted his men, spent hours searching and hoping, and spent countless taxpayer dollars in a seemingly fruitless effort to find the culprit.

He could hear the *click clack, click clack* of the shoes marching in toward his office. He cradled his hurt fist in his left hand, hoping no one would notice the blue bruise forming around the knuckles. He was sure he'd broken his hand with that release earlier in the locker room.

When he looked up, he saw the Sheriff making his way closer and closer to him. He stood, greeted the Chief of Detectives and the Sheriff, and closed the door.

Cops stood around, trying to act busy, but they couldn't help but overhear some of the ramblings and rantings being shouted on the other side of that wooden door.

Ten, maybe fifteen minutes later, the door opened and everyone but Leland stepped out. Keeping their heads high, they rounded the corner and were gone. The only sound in the squad room was the same clicking of shoes growing farther and farther away in the distance.

"Celeste? Come in, please?"

Leland was a kind man, despite his muscular build. He stood at six feet tall and weighed nearly three hundred pounds. His dark, ruddy complexion completed the whole cop look for him. He was one man no one cared to mess with, except of course, for the Sheriff and sometimes the Chief.

Celeste walked gracefully through the room as every eye was on her. A few of the policeman felt a pang of envy. Leland was calling on her more and more often as their views and opinions seemed to get swept under the rug.

When she entered the detective's office, she closed the door and sat next to him. The relationship between them had grown stronger and was becoming much more casual.

"We need a new angle. Any ideas?"

Celeste did have a few. She was taking a more active interest in the case every day. She had done her share of research on this case as well as others. She was reading criminal records and crime novels on her days off and even sat through a few court cases for fun.

"Yes, sir. I do," she responded.

"Let's hear 'em then." Leland was all ears and ready to close the book on this case.

Celeste took a deep breath, allowing her long, dark hair to flow away from her small shoulders. She had been brainstorming all morning and was hoping Leland would ask for her help.

"A candlelight vigil." She spoke with a sense of sureness and confidence. Leland raised an eyebrow at her as she continued.

"I've read a lot lately and I've studied this case almost as much as you have. Sometimes, when a family holds a vigil to honor or remember a victim, it draws the responsible party out. His curiosity gets the better of him and he has to attend. If he was in any way responsible for Trish Colbert's death, he has a warped mind already. I mean, what was the point in shaving her bald and cutting off her poor ear?"

Leland sat and listened patiently.

"If it's the same man, he'll want to come out. He'll want to see the look on their faces, smile at their pain."

"So, that settles it. Would you be willing to contact the Colbert family and set it up?"

"I'd be honored, sir." Celeste was proud and relieved that he would ask for her help again. "Besides, I feel really bad that my last idea got you in a world of trouble."

"Nonsense. That's not your fault. You were right in finding a pattern. Now, let's get this ball rolling."

Chapter Nineteen

Belinda and Carl Colbert stood on the steps of the Anson County courthouse. A large crowd had turned out for the vigil. Belinda could feel her stomach wrench into a knot as she surveyed the masses.

Detective Leland had spoken to them both beforehand and explained the plan. There were undercover cops stationed throughout the crowd and no uniformed officers in sight.

As the glow from so many candles flickered around, Belinda began her prepared speech.

"Thank you all for coming. Trish was a very sweet and loving young woman. She would also appreciate this turn out. Trish always said that there is good in everyone."

She could feel fresh tears forming in her eyes as she swallowed hard and continued. "If only that were true. If there was good in everyone, Trish would be alive today and there would be no need for this candlelight service."

Carl took over from there. "Please help us find Trish's killer. It's all we have left to fight for. We must see the person who killed our daughter brought to justice. If you know anything, anything at all that might help us do that, I'm begging you now. Help Trish rest in peace."

When Carl broke down, Belinda once again took over by leading the crowd in singing "Amazing Grace". Everyone was singing. Well, almost everyone. Freddy Lee just walked around from person to person watching their sad and pathetic faces. They were so lost. Freddy thought about how sad that was. They were caught up in something that didn't even matter now. Only he knew the truth. He and his girls.

Another thought occurred to him. If Trish hadn't been so full of fight, she would be safe now waiting for him to come home. She could've been happy with his family, but instead, she was in the ground, six feet under for no reason.

Oh well, too bad, Freddy thought. When he spied Detective Leland in the crowd, he made his way to him.

"Detective, how are you?" Freddy asked.

"I've been better, Fredlee. Just wanting justice so bad. For those poor people up there." Mark Leland motioned toward the courthouse steps.

"I know what you mean. So, there aren't any leads at all?"

"Nothing we can make official."

"What about the article in the paper? I thought you'd finally found the freak."

"Well, Fredlee, that was a trick. It was supposed to bring 'em out of the woodwork, but he's a smart one. This man is smart."

"Oh, that's a shame." Freddy was bubbling over inside, but had learned from years of practice to control his composure.

"Yes, it is, a shame. A damn shame," Leland agreed. As Leland nodded, he spit in the dirt where he stood. Both men watched as the spittle made a little river of mud and rolled near Freddy's foot. He made a step to his right, avoiding the saliva.

"Well, is this supposed to bring him out of the woodwork, too?"

"We were hoping it might. But so far, we haven't seen anyone who looks suspicious or guilty."

"Yeah, I haven't seen anyone I don't recognize," Freddy commented. "Well, I should head home. I have to take a course at Maxwell starting tomorrow. Gotta get up early."

"Is that right? What kind of course, Fredlee?"

"Boring stuff, Mr. Leland. Just one class that's been added since I graduated. It's only for one semester, but I have to take it to keep the business going. Without it, I'd lose my license to practice. I don't want that to happen."

"Oh, me either. Ain't nobody around can do what you do. You do a great job, Fredlee, just like your dad always did."

"Thank you, sir. I appreciate that. Hey, if you're around tomorrow night, I've got Mrs. Hildreth. She passed away in her sleep night before last."

"Is that so? I sure hate to hear that. Mrs. Hildreth was my second grade teacher."

"I had her, too. She was a dear. But, she lived a long life and went peaceful."

"What time's visitation?"

"Seven to nine. Come on by. She had a small family, so I doubt if there will be a long line. And you can see what all I've done to the place. New carpeting, lighter paint, and all new furnishings."

"Way to go, Fredlee!" Leland exclaimed. "Your father sure would be proud of you. I hated it for you and Mrs. Carolyn when he passed. He was a good man, your father."

Freddy smiled graciously and shook Leland's hand. "I appreciate that, sir. Maybe I'll see you tomorrow night?"

"Maybe. I'll try my best." Leland nodded and watched as Freddy walked away.

He might be an odd young man, but it's too bad there aren't more honest and hardworking men like that around these days. Fredlee sure has grown up to be a fine gentleman. Leland was thrown from his thoughts when Celeste approached.

"I haven't seen a thing. Have you?" she asked.

Leland shook his head and looked on at the Colbert family. The singing was done and they had just asked for a minute of complete silence to end the event. When it was over, Celeste looked to Leland with tears in her eyes. The wax from her candle had just started to drip over the paper cone that held it in place.

"Sooner or later, he'll screw up. And when he does, you'll catch him," she said, attempting to comfort Leland.

Leland thought about her comment for a moment. "Yeah, but I'm worried it will be later. I can't have another missing girl. Not on my watch, Celeste."

Part Two: Ellen

Chapter Twenty

1977

The Bee Gees sang out to *Stayin' Alive* as Freddy viewed himself in the mirror.

Not too bad, Freddy, not too bad.

His hair had grown longer, just touching his shoulders and he thought of his newly trimmed sideburns as far out. He moved his head back and forth with the beat of the music and even spun around, doing his best John Travolta moves.

Oh, yeah, baby. I'm down with it.

"Oh, Freddy! You look fab!" he heard Lori say. She was still in bed, resting after an all-night lovemaking session with Michelle by her side. Lisa had gone to her own room. Paula and Amber shared a room. But his lovely Lori was with him day and night. He could never be too far from her.

"Do you really think so, Lori?"

"Why, yes, I do. So, are you ready?"

Four months earlier, Freddy had received an official letter from Raleigh. He plopped down on the sofa next to Lori as he read it first to himself, then to her. Reading it a second time confirmed the meaning. It read:

Dear Mr. Fred Argus Lee Junior,

We are informing you, that according to our records, the state of North Carolina has added a required course for mortuary school that you have yet to complete. In order to maintain an active and valid license, you are hereby obligated to fulfill this mandate. You may contact the main office of the Coroner's School in Raleigh, N.C. for assistance if needed. Thank you and best of luck with your career.

Sincerely,

Governor William A. Beasley

Freddy had called the main office as suggested in the letter and found that the one course, gerontology, was offered at Maxwell University, the closet to his home. He would drive back and forth again, as he had so many times before, but after getting accepted and paying the tuition, he was ready.

"I'm going to miss you, sweet cheeks. You be good while I'm gone and maybe I'll bring you home a prize soon."

Freddy winked at Lori and felt an immediate rush. This woman was everything he could ever hope to have and so much more. Lori winked back, in Freddy's mind.

She was head over heels in love with this man and blushed as she remembered the night before. He really did bring out the animal in her and all his girls.

"I'll be good, I promise," Lori said in a sultry voice.

Freddy moved her to the edge of the bed and sat next to her. He gave her a long and passionate kiss, then stood and headed out the door. He was still singing *Stayin' Alive* as he backed out of the drive and headed to Maxwell.

* * * * * * * *

Ellen Kelly was excited and a little pensive as she loaded up her car. The Caprice Classic was shining in the early September sun. Her trunk was packed full and she was throwing one last bag in the back seat.

"You'll call as soon as you get there?"

"Yes, mom. Don't I always?" Ellen rolled her eyes before turning to face her mother.

"I can't help it. I worry. The world is full of bad people, you know?"

"I know. I know to keep my doors locked. Don't talk to strangers. Don't take rides from strangers and don't ever, ever accept their candy."

Ellen's mom smiled and gave her a tight hug. "Someday you'll be a mother and you'll worry, too."

"Mom! I'm nineteen. I know how to take care of myself!"

Betsy hugged her daughter for a moment longer. Ellen was in her sophomore year at Maxwell University, but she worried over her only girl now just like she did when she went on her first date.

She was a mature young woman and Betsy was very proud. She knew Ellen could care for herself, but there was always danger out there that young people just don't see.

They see danger in nothing! she thought as Ellen got in the car. Betsy gave her daughter a wave and stood watching until Ellen was out of sight.

She shivered in the cool autumn air and heard her two sons screaming at each other. Going back in, she had to separate the two boys. They were fighting over the Atari, again. Betsy pulled them apart, went into the kitchen and started cleaning up. The best way to keep from worrying about Ellen was to stay busy.

As soon as she was out of sight, Ellen pulled out her hidden pack of Marlboros and lit one. She exhaled a nice, slow breath. It was the first cigarette she'd had all day. If her mom smelled smoke on her, she would have beaten her. Nineteen or not, she was still a tyrant of a parent and smoking was totally against the rules.

She had been sneaking out to her brothers' tree house all summer to catch a puff here and there and had been hiding them in a small flowerpot. *Shit! I forgot the flowerpot. If Gaige or Daniel find it and tell mom, so help me I'll kick their skinny little butts.*

As she entered the first town, she slowed down and forgot about the butts. Traffic was worse now than it had been in June, the last time she'd been on this road. She thought that with summer over, the traffic would have died down by now.

She turned on the radio, finding *The Way I Feel Tonight* by the Bay City Rollers, her favorite group. She sang along as she drove on.

Two hours later, after singing along to every song on BIG 78.9, she was back at school. Campus was crawling with freshmen, trying to find their way around the big school. And then there were the seniors, their heads in the air. Ellen would fit in between them all as a second year veteran here.

She knew the campus well, but was still not confident enough to really be alone. She was sharing a dorm room again this year and was nervous to see who she would be stuck living with.

She wheeled around to her dorm building, Bushmere Hall, put a parking pass in place on the mirror and stood to stretch. She gazed up at the tall stack of dorms, and counted up to the fifth floor. That was hers, room 508.

Another young girl bumped in to her and caught her off guard.

"Oh, I'm sorry," the girl said.

"No problem," retorted Ellen.

As she headed up to her room, she noticed the girl going there, too.

"Are you Ellen?" the girl asked.

"Yep, and you must be Cathy."

Cathy smiled and held out her arms. "It's nice to meet you, Ellen."

"Same to you. So, we're roommates, huh?"

"Looks that way."

Ellen and Cathy started unpacking and soon they had their dorm in tip-top shape. Ellen placed a strobe light on a table between the beds.

"Far out!" Cathy shouted.

When Cathy hung her Les McKeown poster, Ellen knew that they were going to be great friends. They both loved the same band and both admired the same member of that band, *The Bay City Rollers*.

On the other side of campus, Freddy walked to the registrar's office. He handed over the paperwork and explained that he would be commuting. He was given the parking pass he needed and given the schedule for his class. Upon reading it, he headed to Kiser Hall, the building where most mortuary and undergraduate med classes were held.

After a long day, Ellen flopped down on her twin size bed. She was exhausted and classes wouldn't even start for two more days. She fell asleep and dreamed of crowded classes, cute boys and Stuart Wood, another member of the same band. A hard knock on her door woke her. She stumbled to the door and pulled it open.

"Ellen? Your mom is on the phone."

"Be right there." Ellen closed her eyes and frowned to herself. She'd forgotten to call her.

"Hi, mom! I'm sorry!"

"You forgot to call me. I was frantic. I was calling the police if you weren't there."

"I said I'm sorry. I was just tired and fell asleep after I unpacked. I'm fine, I promise."

Betsy took a deep breath. "Well, I'm just glad you made it safely. How was your drive?"

Ellen could barely hear her mother over the noise. Girls were talking wildly, yelling and laughing. Ellen looked around smiling. She loved college life. But her mom was going to drive her crazy with worry before she could ever graduate.

"It was fine. Just long and lonely."

"You know, your father and I could have driven you. At least you would have had company."

"Yes, I know. But I love having a car and—"

"Freedom," Betsy finished her sentence.

She and Harold had heard it over and over all summer until finally they caved to Ellen's begging. They were going to worry about her no matter what. Ellen had accepted that, so she took another course on self-defense during the summer just to satisfy them.

"Well, I know you're busy and I won't keep you," Betsy said. She really didn't want to hang up. It was nice hearing Ellen's voice on the other end.

"Okay, I'll call you tomorrow." Ellen hung up after saying goodbye and that she loved her mom, too.

This is going to be a long semester, she thought to herself. *A very long semester.*

Chapter Twenty-One

Ellen's head was throbbing. She struggled through Philosophy with her very first hangover. The professor was going on and on and in her mind, all she heard blah, blah, blah, blah. She couldn't wait for this to be over.

One more class, Accounting 102, and she'd be done and could sleep this off, maybe. She had to study for a Trig test and get a jump-start on an essay in Great American Authors before she could truly relax. Then, the weekend could officially start.

Betsy and Harold were not very pleased with her decision to stay on campus this weekend, but Maxwell was playing Western and she really wanted to be here for the celebration. School had been a crazy place for weeks with March Madness promising to bring a lot more excitement, and Maxwell was doing great so far. They had made it through two rounds and were to face Western on Saturday. If she could just get through the next day and a half, the party could start.

As she trudged across campus to the Accounting department a tall, thin man walked towards her. He was wearing face paint and half of his face was white, while the other half was green, the college colors. His fluffy, green afro could be seen from a mile away, Ellen thought.

As he neared her, someone yelled out, *"Western is going down, people!"*

The man dressed in college pride shouted out, "Yeah, baby!" and gave his fists a pump up and down.

The screams made Ellen jump. She wasn't usually jumpy at all. In fact, she was normally calm and cool. Her stomach was turning flips and when she belched, she could taste the strong spirits from last night's party.

Note to self: Ellen Kelly will never, ever drink beer and vodka in the same night again. Second note to self: Ellen Kelly will not drink anything during the school week ever, ever again. On second thought, just don't drink again, kid. No more alcohol for this college sophomore ever, ever again.

She rolled her eyes and continued on.

Before she could reach the Accounting department, she began to heave. It only took two more full heaves and she was vomiting all over the concrete steps leading up to the classrooms. She stood there gagging and heaving and the more she gagged, the more she heaved.

"Check it out, dude! That chick is totally barfing!" said one guy. Another started laughing and imitating her disgusting sounds. Ellen could feel her cheeks reddening, but was too sick to care at that moment.

"I think you could use some water. That might be more your speed. What ya think?" Ellen heard.

She raised up to see a dark haired, very handsome man standing over her with a cup of water. She didn't speak, only took the water and began to down every drop.

"Whoa! Slow down or that'll come back up, too," he advised.

Ellen did as he recommended and took the time to thank him.

"No prob, Ellen Kelly."

"How did you know my name?"

The young man laughed. "I see you every day! We have trig together."

Ellen was really embarrassed now. "I'm sorry. I try to stay focused in there. Trig is hard this semester."

The boy began to nod. "Peter Helder, at your service, ma'am, as he held his hand out to her.

"Ellen Kelly, well, you totally know that already. I'm so totally humiliated." Her cheeks were now a dark rosy shade of blush.

"Don't be so shy. We all bork when we've had too much. I take it you were at Thom's party last night?"

"Yeah, but don't remind me."

Peter smiled softly and Ellen could see a row of straight, white teeth behind a set of well-shaped lips.

"So, where you headed now, Ellen Kelly?"

"Accounting. And I dread it more than ever now," she mumbled.

"I'll be in the cafeteria at twelve. Save you a seat?"

"I don't think I could possibly eat anything."

Peter laughed loudly. "Well, you don't have to eat to grace my table, do you?"

Ellen could feel herself growing redder by the minute. "I suppose I could join you."

"Far out! I'll see you then. Feel better and good luck with the numbers!" Peter turned back to see Ellen climbing the steps, all fifteen of them.

She waved back to him and made it into the class without any more heaving.

After class, she made her way to the cafeteria. She saw Peter standing near the door and smiled. When he noticed her, he gave a wave. His height made his head seem two feet above everyone else.

They sat together during the hour Peter had between classes and the two of them shared their likes and dislikes about college life. Ellen found talking to Peter much easier than most of the other boys on campus. He seemed more mature and refined. He was a senior, so that made sense she supposed.

When the hour was up, Peter walked Ellen back to her dorm and gave her a gentle hug goodbye. Ellen had about two, maybe three hours of work and she'd be done for the weekend. Her stomach was feeling much better and her head was finally done throbbing.

Once she was back in her room, she opened her trig book and began practicing problems she'd struggled with. Her eyes grew heavy and she began to nod. Soon, she was sound asleep.

Cathy walked in, slammed the door and Ellen jumped as she lifted her heavy head. "Noise! Too much noise!" Ellen grumbled.

"Sorry, girl. But it's the weekend! Get up and get moving! We've got a party to attend!"

Ellen gave a half grin, rolled her eyes and replied. "I'm too tired. I think I'll stay in tonight."

"But I can't go alone. I promised my mom I'd use the buddy system since that asshole Ted Bundy escaped again. You have to go. Pleeease?"

Cathy used her most pathetic beg until finally, Ellen relented and said she'd go. "But no drinking tonight, okay? Really, Cathy, I just can't."

"Fine. Totally. I can dig that. You can be a stiff if you wanna be. But I'm getting lucky in every way tonight, baby!"

Ellen didn't care what Cathy wanted. She'd humiliated herself on the steps of the accounting building, been too nervous and fidgety to eat while Peter gulped down an entire cheeseburger, fries and cookies in less than ten minutes, and was still hung over from last night.

She was showering and singing *The Way I Feel Tonight* when she began to recall her last Sunday morning at home. Her mom had cooked a huge breakfast and she and her family had eaten together. Daniel and Gaige argued the entire time about some meaningless video game, her dad read the paper, and Betsy had eaten silently as Ellen gazed at her.

"Mom? What's the matter?"

Betsy responded in a far off, dreamy way about how she wished Ellen could have picked a college closer to town.

"Mom, not that again. I'm very happy at Maxwell. It's a great school and you know that. Plus, I'm getting classes there that aren't offered at Tech. Why do you put this guilt trip on me every time I come home?"

Harold slid the newspaper over to the right of his plate.

"Don't mind your mom, Ellen. She's just lonesome. I keep telling her she needs a hobby to keep her busy."

"I don't need a hobby, Harold Kelly. I need my daughter closer to home."

"Geez, mom! I'm so totally not discussing this again, like, totally not now."

Ellen took a deep breath and let it out very loudly. The sound seemed to echo through the now quiet kitchen.

Daniel began to mock his sister. "Yeah, like, totally, mom."

"Shut up, you little dweeb!" Ellen retorted.

"Make me," Daniel came back.

Then Gaige had to put in his two cents worth. "Make him, Ellen, please!"

A swift kick under the table from Daniel shut him up quickly.

"Ouch!"

"Now you shut up!"

"Totally, shut up. Like, yesterday."

Back and forth Daniel and Gaige teased one another until finally, Ellen had pushed away from the table.

"I'm so not doing this." She hurriedly took the stairs up to her room.

She could still hear her brothers yelling at each other even with the door shut. Harold then began to make noise as he chastised both boys. The dishes clanking in the sink told Ellen her mom was washing up their breakfast mess. She should help her. After all, breakfast was really delicious. But she was so angry with her.

Betsy had a way of making anyone feel guilty about anything at any time. Ellen resented that, but loved her mom dearly. When Betsy knocked on the door, Ellen told her to come in.

"I'm sorry, Ellie. I truly am. I don't want you to feel sad about being away. I just worry about you. You're so young and there is so much meanness in our world. I just want to put you in a bubble and glue you inside."

Ellen thought she understood, but she really didn't. "I know, mom. I just really like it there and I'm happy. I want you to be happy, too."

"I'll be happy when you walk across the stage and the dean hands you that degree."

Betsy brushed through Ellen's hair and smiled at her only daughter. "Just promise me you'll be safe?"

"You know I always am."

They hugged tightly, and then Betsy started helping Ellen pack for the trip back to school. They laughed, talked, and shared secrets. Ellen really enjoyed that and was relieved to have her mom content when she pulled out the drive two hours later.

Now, she was standing in the shower, thinking of how she missed the noise of home, the warm fire Harold was sure to have blazing by now, and the smells coming from the kitchen as Betsy whipped up wonderful meals.

She even missed those little dorks she called brothers. Daniel and Gaige were her brothers and it was her job to torture them. But if anyone else did, she would have gone into attack mode. They felt the same about her. They admired Ellen, but would never want her to know that, but she already did.

She decided that next weekend, she would give them a surprise visit. She would just show up and they would be so thrilled to see her.

Chapter Twenty-Two

Cathy and Ellen could hear KISS blasting *Rock n Roll All Night* as they neared the frat house where the latest party was being hosted. When the door opened, smoked rolled out and the smell of beer and whiskey rushed through Ellen's nostrils. She wasn't in the mood for this night, but had promised Cathy.

Cathy yelled out to someone across the room and left Ellen standing there alone.

Great. I'm at a party I didn't want to attend and now I'm all alone.

"I wasn't sure you'd make it," Ellen heard someone speak.

She turned, looked up and standing with his head in a string of green flags and white lights was Peter.

"Hi! I didn't know you were coming," she shouted over the noise.

"After this morning, I'm surprised to see you," Peter teased.

"Trust me, I'm staying clear of all alcohol tonight."

"You shouldn't drink, anyway. A bright and talented woman like you doesn't need her senses dulled by something so lame."

195

Normally, Ellen would have agreed by saying *totally*, but she softly smiled and could feel the blush returning to her cheeks.

"I love the way you blush, Ellen. And your smile is adorable."" Peter inched closer to her and she could feel his breath on her neck. The sensation was maddening.

As the song changed over to *I'm in You,* Peter began to sing. His voice was remarkably close to that of the Peter singing the song on the stereo.

Ellen giggled a little girl kind of giggle and looked down. Peter was staring at her as he sang and she could feel the awkwardness filling the air around them. Moments later, he was placing the edge of her face in his hand and pulling her into him. The kiss he gave was soft and sweet.

The night dragged on as Ellen and Peter talked and laughed. When the last of the partygoers had either stumbled back to their own dorms or passed out somewhere in the house, Ellen noticed that she and Peter were basically alone in the room. The music had quieted and only an occasional moan or heave from a kid nearby broke through the silence.

"Oh my goodness! Cathy! Where is she? I'm supposed to be her buddy for the night!"

Peter slid as close to Ellen as he could, wrapped his arm tightly around her and whispered in her ear.

"I think your buddy got lucky. We're all alone."

His kisses were still soft, but filled with an intense passion that Ellen felt shoot through her entire body.

Peter held her for another hour until finally he offered to walk her home. She really didn't want to leave or let this night end, but she nodded as Peter stood and offered his hand. When they were back at Bushmere Hall, Peter told Ellen how much he'd enjoyed the night with her.

"Yeah, totally. It's been really great."

"I don't want to leave," Peter whined like a child. He took a deep breath, gave Ellen one last kiss, and walked away. Ellen watched as his tall body became nothing more than a distant silhouette.

Cathy wasn't home, but that wasn't much of a surprise to Ellen. She snuggled up in bed, turned on her disco light, and let the colored patterns on the walls and ceiling lull her to sleep. Cathy came tiptoeing in an hour later. When Ellen rolled over, she squinted through sleepy eyes and noticed the clock's red square numbers. It was five A.M.

Cathy cried out in a long, dreamy sigh, waiting for Ellen to ask about her night. When she finally did, she told Ellen all about the boy she'd met. All about how good-looking he was, how smart he was, how mature he was. This boy was the man of her dreams. She could just tell. Ellen stuck her finger in her mouth and acted as if she'd gag. The two girls laughed and whispered and eventually they both fell asleep.

Freddy stood in the parking lot and watched as the lights waned and waxed from outside her window.

Two hundred miles away, in a small town called Oakdale, Betsy Kelly had found a hobby. She plundered through bins of clothes and held up a top that she thought Ellen might like.

"How much?"

The woman sitting behind the table answered with "a quarter."

Betsy smiled as she looked through the pile of household appliances on the table. Before she left, she had found Daniel a Led Zeppelin eight-track, two tops for Ellen, a great looking pair of pants for Gaige, even a saw blade for Harold, something she knew he'd been needing.

As for herself, she had a Bundt pan, some earrings, and an iron. She loved this thing called *yard sales*. She had only spent two dollars and had all this to show for it. She couldn't wait to show Ellen.

The next stop was at Rose's department store. She had a million things she needed to pick up. The boys had promised Ellen they'd watch Maxwell play Western and she wanted lots of snacks.

Ellen would be in the crowd of fans, so even she would watch this game. When she left, she turned on the radio to hear that dreadful band KISS, and immediately turned the dial. Only kids liked them and for the life of her, she couldn't figure out why. She settled on the quiet as she drove home.

Pulling in the drive, she noticed Daniel and Gaige out playing basketball together.

Maybe this is the day they decide to actually be friends, Betsy hoped.

Both boys came over to help her with her bags and she excitedly told them about their yard sale items. Of course, they fought over the eight-track and Gaige didn't even like the pants.

Such is life.

Someday, her boys would grow close, but it wouldn't start today. Harold thanked Betsy for his blade and set out to his workshop to install it.

All day, Betsy worked hard to clean the house. She even tidied up Ellen's room, finding a hidden pack of cigarettes in a shoebox on her shelf. She shook her head as she bent each one, watching it crumble into the trash.

That evening, the family sat down together in the den and the game started soon after. They looked hard at every shot as the camera passed through the crowd of cheering teens hoping to catch a glimpse of Ellen. With ten minutes left on the clock ending the first half, they saw her.

"Look! There she is!" Daniel yelled. They all clapped and cheered at the site of their pretty girl. Sitting beside her was Cathy, her roommate.

Cathy had visited with Ellen once already this year so they recognized her right away. To the right of Ellen was a man that looked to be at least twenty-two, maybe older. His arm was around Ellen and in the split second that they saw her, he leaned over to give her a kiss.

"Oh, that's just sick!" Gaige mumbled.

"Gross!" Daniel added.

"Who in the world was *that*?" Harold asked.

"I'm sure I don't know," Betsy chimed.

They grew quiet as they wondered.

Freddy sat directly behind Ellen. He was alone tonight, but he didn't care. He had Ellen in his sights and that's all that mattered. This was the one. The one that would make Lori happier than any of her other friends had made her.

He became aroused as he thought of having Ellen on his metal worktable, strapped helplessly and begging for her life. He felt a surge of excitement as he pictured her bald and earless and pleading to go free. The image of her eyes growing wild with fear as she saw Lori for the first time made his heart skip a beat.

It wouldn't be long now.

When the game was over and Western had all but crushed Maxwell, the fans began to file out of the gym, silently wishing they'd won. Peter held on to Ellen tightly as they made it back to Bushmere. One soft kiss was all she got tonight. They were tired and both ready for sleep.

"See you tomorrow?" Peter asked in a low voice.

Ellen nodded. "I'd like that."

Peter waved and walked away across the campus.

Freddy stood in the shadows watching her. He wanted to plan this one just right. He had no room for errors now. Police were searching in vain for several missing women, and there was a serial killer stalking young brunettes up and down the east coast and as far west as the Rockies.

Women everywhere had their guards up and were learning self -defense. They were being told almost daily to never go anywhere alone and to always have a flashlight, a whistle, or something to help attract help if a situation arose.

Freddy despised that freak, Bundy. He was putting a real kink in his perfect plan and he really didn't like being underestimated. He was a nothing, a nobody.

Ted Bundy was a jerk that didn't know how to appreciate a real woman for her beauty. Freddy was an artist. He took great pride in his work and the final results. He could never just throw away a perfectly good girl.

He thought of Trish, how he had thrown her away, and No Name, still stuck in the attic, but they weren't *perfectly good girls*. They didn't deserve Freddy. He knew that.

Bundy, on the other hand, tossed women to the side like garbage all of the time. He truly was a sick man. Freddy was glad he had more sense about him than that.

His mind wondered back to Lori. He would drive home again tonight as he did every night. But the semester would soon end and he'd have this damned class behind him.

Too many things were distracting him now. He had to remain focused on his goal or else he'd ruin everything and only have himself to truly blame.

Chapter Twenty-Three

Ellen knew that she was quickly falling in love. She was almost asleep when the girl across the hall, Annie, knocked on her door.

"Telephone, Ellen!"

Ellen groaned as she stepped out into the dimly lit hallway. She knew it would be her brothers, probably calling to rub her nose in the fact that her college team didn't make it to the Sweet Sixteen.

"Hello?"

"Hi, sweetie! We saw you on T.V.!" Betsy almost sang with excitement.

"Yeah? I didn't know they showed me. We lost, you know?"

"I'm sorry, dear. But you had fun, didn't you?"

"I did. Until the last ten seconds of the game, anyway."

"What I mean is you had fun with your new friend. What's his name?"

It took Ellen a second to know that they must have seen his arm around her during her five seconds of fame. "Oh, that was just Peter. He's a friend."

"Friends don't kiss on the mouth in public, Ellen Kelly."

"Mom. We met a few nights ago and he's very sweet. He's a senior and very smart. I think you and dad would like him."

"A few nights ago? You met him a few nights ago and you're kissing him on the mouth?"

Ellen placed a hand over the receiver as she groaned. She hated the way Betsy tried to control her, even from a two hundred mile distance. And she loathed Betsy's old-fashioned ideas.

Other girls had moms that spoke of free love, and making love, not war. But not her mother. Her mother was raised to be prim and proper. And apparently, waiting for marriage to kiss.

"Mom. I'm sleepy and very tired. It's been a busy few days. I want to go to bed. Anything else you need to fuss at me for?"

"I'm not fussing, Ellie. I just wanted to know who this man is. Your brothers saw that kiss, you know?"

Ellen smiled at that thought. She could hear them as plainly as if she had heard it herself. The way they probably gagged themselves and carried on about how gross it was.

"Okay. So they know their nineteen-year-old sister kissed a boy. Is it that bad, mom?"

Another girl, Kim, walked by and made a smacking sound with her lips. Ellen was probably the only girl in college not sexually active and her mom was making a fuss over a kiss?

Betsy Kelly would die if she knew what all the other girls were doing, many of them right at that very moment, and it was a lot more than kissing. She should be proud of her daughter, but instead, she was yakking away about a peck on the mouth.

"I'm hanging up now, mom. Go to bed. It's late."

Betsy was trying to say *wait! Your daddy wants to talk to you*, but Ellen placed the receiver back on the cradle and took a deep breath.

That woman is going to drive me insane before I can graduate and get married!

Betsy was still holding the phone. "Ellen? Ellen? Are you there?" When there was no reply, she put her phone down, too. She stood staring at the orange thing, hoping it would ring again and Ellen would apologize for hanging up. But instead, Ellen was already back in bed, dreaming about the day when she and Peter would actually do *it*.

He was a gentleman, that much she knew. And she also knew that was a good thing. She didn't always agree with her mother, but she had been raised with morals and self-respect.

The whole idea of wild girls made her wonder where Cathy was. She'd left the gym with a different guy, someone Ellen had not seen before.

What is Cathy doing tonight?

Betsy turned to Harold, who had turned the dial on the television to the local news.

"Well?"

"Well, what, Betsy?" Harold craned his neck to watch the news and Betsy stepped a little more to her right, blocking the screen completely.

"What do you mean, 'well what, Betsy'? Our daughter is making out with a stranger and you're not upset in the least? There is a serial killer out there, Harold!"

Harold sighed. "Ellen is very smart and independent, Betsy. She's fine. You have got to stop worrying about her all the time. She knows what she's doing. And besides that, it was a little kiss. Nothing sinful about it. Relax." As he spoke, he patted the empty spot on the couch next to him. He really wasn't in the mood to cuddle his wife, but anything to get her to move away from the T.V.

She eased down beside him and Harold placed an arm around her. He squeezed her gently as they watched the weather forecast. The next story was an update on the Bundy case. It was on every station and when he stood to change the channel, Betsy didn't argue.

Daniel and Gaige were already upstairs talking about the game. They had already forgotten about the kiss. At twelve and thirteen, it just wasn't worth remembering, especially since it was their sister...*gross*.

Chapter Twenty-Four

Freddy could feel his eyes growing heavier and heavier. The sound of a car horn startled him just before he skidded off the roadside into a bank of snow.

The winter was the harshest he ever remembered experiencing and the long drive home each day didn't help. His class was held from four P.M until six P.M. and by the time he arrived home, it was usually at least ten. The class wasn't too boring, but he was sleepy now.

As cars sped by him, he roused a little and flipped on the radio. Mashing buttons to navigate from one station to another, he found nothing but commercials. His eyes were only off the road a second, but looking back over the steering wheel, he saw three deer directly in his path. He slammed on the brakes, felt the car fish tailing, and began to circle around and around in the road. The deer ran off into the cold dark night. Freddy sat there without moving until he realized he was fine. The car was still on the road and undamaged.

Not cool, Freddy, not cool.

His heart was racing. He knew at that moment he couldn't possibly drive another mile on the slick road. He was just too tired. He pulled over lower to the ditch, pushed the gear shifter up to park and turned off the lights. Freddy snuggled down under his coat and thought of Lori.

The girls will be so worried. I should find a place to call. Lori will be beside herself.

He was a little unnerved about Ellen Kelly, too. So far, he wanted her worse than he had all the others, except of course, for Lori.

He was nodding off to sleep with Ellen on his mind when there was a knock on his window.

"Are you okay, sir?"

Freddy looked up to see a young woman bending down to his window.

"I saw the skid marks in the road and figured you lost control. Too cold out to be stuck. You need a ride?"

He pushed himself up and immediately had the craziest idea. "Thank you. You and your husband are very kind to stop for me."

"No husband. Just me and the open road."

Freddy smiled. "Well, I think I'll be okay, but maybe if you followed me for a ways, just to be sure."

The woman nodded. "Sure thing. I'll be right behind you."

Freddy yelled thanks over the falling snow. The only sound around for miles was the windshield wipers swooshing back and forth, back and forth. Freddy cranked up the Impala's engine, shifted to drive and flipped on his headlights. He drove especially slow as he rounded the curve ahead.

Think Freddy, think. How to get that sweet, young woman in the car with me?

He drove for about a half mile, and then switched on his turn signal. He gently took the car to the right and stopped. When the woman emerged from her car, he held the door open.

"Something's knocking under the hood. I'm going to turn on the engine, you see if you hear it, too."

"Okay, crank 'er up."

He did and she stood there, still and silent.

"Um, I don't hear a thing."

"I'm going to take a look. Would you sit here and listen? Maybe you'll hear it from inside. I might can wiggle a few wires while you rev the engine."

The woman was happy to oblige. She stepped over, Freddy stood, and she got in. As soon as she was in, he grabbed her by the hair and with a tight fist, hit her across the jaw. She went down fast.

Well, well, well. The broken down car ruse still works, huh, Freddy?

Freddy looked around briefly, then pushed the woman's limp body over and sat back down. He shifted the car back into drive and continued on.

He was wide awake now. He watched the woman's own headlights become smaller and smaller as he drove. It was that simple to get a naïve, trusting woman into your car.

When the woman woke, they were about twenty miles south of where her car had been deserted.

"What did you do?"

Freddy shouted out a *haaah,* sounding between a maddened laugh and a sigh.

"I'm Freddy Lee, don't you know who I am?"

The woman shook her head in fear as Freddy continued to laugh.

"Well, that's cool. You see, there is so much hype right now about that Bundy character, I've remained incognito. But there are too many differences between me and him to even try to compare."

"What do you want? Money? Sex? I'll do whatever you want. Just don't hurt me, please. I was only trying to help you. Don't hurt me, okay?"

"I'm not going to hurt you, dearie. Honest. That's not my style. And trust me. Sex is the last thing on my mind right now. So, what's your name?"

"I'm Cathy Mills. I'm a student at Maxwell U."

Freddy looked at Cathy again and studied her face.

"Oh, yeah! I know you. You're Ellen's roomy!"

"You know Ellen?"

"Sure I do! She's coming home with me soon, too! How perfect. How absolutely perfect this is."

Cathy felt the apprehension building. "Why would Ellen come home with you?"

"Because I chose her. Lori already knows all about her and is so excited to meet her. She will be ecstatic to meet you, too."

"Chose her?"

"Yep. She is special because she spoke to me. In my mind she spoke to me. I heard her clear as a bell. She said *Take me, Freddy. Please choose me.* So I did. And now you two can be with Lori and me forever!"

Cathy sat quietly for the remaining trip. She looked frantically at every stop sign, traffic light, and intersection, hoping there would be someone that might hear her scream. But on a cold, snowy night like this, no one was out aside from them.

All the way home, Freddy talked to her. He didn't seem to notice that she wasn't responding. He told her all about Lori and the others and never looked to see her tears streaming down her cheeks.

As he told her the story about how he and Lori met and how the other girls had come to be with him, Cathy sobbed. She was desperate for a plan to escape, but the car was moving too quickly and at every stop, he held her hair tightly near the roots.

There was no escape, no way out. They pulled into the drive and Cathy saw that there were several lights on. Freddy talked about Lori the whole way home, and from how it sounded, she was as deranged as he. But maybe there was a chance, even a small one that she would help her out of this mess.

No help came for Cathy as Freddy prepped her the way he had so many times now. And just before he began the final step of embalming Cathy, he brought Lori and Michelle in to meet her. That was the last thing Cathy would see.

Freddy left her in place, strapped to the metal table as he and Lori made love. He couldn't wait to see her. It had been such a long day.

"At least you're home now and we have another friend with us."

Freddy appreciated Lori's words. He held her firmly while the embalming machine finished the procedure that would immortalize Cathy forever.

"That was so good, baby. I needed that so bad."

"I did, too. I've missed you today."

"So, did I miss anything? What did you and the girls do all day?"

Lori responded, saying, "Not much. Watched T.V., talked, listened to music." She sounded dreamy as Freddy listened on intensely.

When the work was all done, he toted his girls one by one into the house and placed them in different positions this time. Michelle and Lisa would sit in the den a while now, Lori sat on the toilet as Freddy showered, Paula was in the kitchen, coffee mug in front of her. Amber lay on the bed in her room.

Because Cathy had such a rough first day, she was resting in the living room. Freddy placed a book in her newly dead hands and turned the lights down low, giving her just enough light to read by, but not too bright to hurt her tired eyes.

Freddy stood watching Cathy before he went up to shower. She wasn't at all what he would have chosen, but she would work. She was too wild, too stained by other men. But now that he had her, he assured her that she would never want another man. He might give her a little of himself someday, but right now he wasn't at all attracted to her.

Cathy looked to her left, where her eyes had in actuality stopped looking at anything. "I understand, Freddy. I do. I'm dirty. But maybe someday you'll find me to be good enough to touch. Maybe soon you'll decide I'm worthy of your love."

"Maybe, Cathy. We'll see." Then Freddy made his way up to where Lori waited.

"When will you bring Ellen home, babe?" she asked.

"Soon. I'm devising a plan. But now that her roommate is gone, she'll be even more cautious. This one will take careful planning. But don't you worry, my love. She'll be joining us soon."

The steam from the shower felt so good against his cold skin. He actually hated this time of year. There had been so much excitement around Christmas. He and the girls had enjoyed a tree trimming party, roasted chestnuts, danced, drank eggnog, and had a terrific time under the pretty lights when the decorating was done.

Freddy watched the excitement in their eyes when he opened their gifts and graciously accepted their hugs and kisses when they saw what he had bought them all. Christmas was wonderful in the Lee home, but after the holiday, Freddy could feel the depression worming its way back into his mind. The cold, the dark and dreary evenings, the bland looking trees and landscape all around; it was too much some days. He had trouble getting out of bed, even with Lori cheering him on. And suddenly, he remembered Carolyn having this same problem.

He stood under the hot water, letting the heat warm him. Lori sang to him. She always knew just what to do. He said, "I love you, Lori. I want you to know that I do. I love you."

"I love you, too, my sweetheart," she replied in a singsong voice.

Chapter Twenty-Five

The sun rose to a rainy, dreary Sunday morning. Ellen lay still listening to the rain splatter against the small window between the beds. It lulled her back to sleep for several more minutes. When she rolled over to hear all about Cathy's adventure from last night, she saw that her bed was still made and Cathy wasn't in it.

She propped up on her shoulders and sighed. Cathy got all the good-looking men. With a well-endowed upper body like she had and her curvy hips, it was easy to understand why. Ellen thought of her own figure. It resembled a toothpick. Maybe a stick. A stick with no branches or leaves to disguise what wasn't there.

Ellen sank back down under the covers. She smiled as she thought about Peter. He liked her, so why was she feeling sorry for herself? Maybe it wasn't self-pity so much as jealousy. When she cracked her eyes open again, the digital clock on the dresser alerted her in block style numbers that it was twelve o'clock noon. Cathy still wasn't home.

After she showered and dressed, she went to the commons area looking for her. There were plenty of other girls, gathered on sofas and sitting two to a chair in one corner. The T.V. was on, the lights were bright, and they were all giggling and laughing. But Cathy wasn't there.

Ellen pulled out her philosophy notes and began to study a little. She looked out the window a little too often, anxiously waiting for Cathy.

When the sun had set, she still wasn't home. Ellen walked back down the hall and asked, "Has anyone seen Cathy? She didn't come home last night. I haven't heard from her."

All the girls that filled the room looked at her and began making comments like, "Lucky Cathy", "I haven't seen her", "Nope. Sorry." Everyone just sort of stared at Ellen until she turned and went back to her room.

She'll come slinking in tonight and tell me all about her wild weekend.

Monday morning, Cathy had still not come home. Ellen sat in the office of campus security, telling the college security guard about what had happened.

"She loves to party on the weekends, but during the week, she works very hard. She's an honor roll student. Cathy takes her student career seriously. Ask her professors, check her G.P.A., I'm telling you, something's wrong."

Security listened to her and took a statement. They would do what they could to locate Cathy, they assured Ellen.

She headed to class, but couldn't shake the feeling that something was wrong, that something bad had happened. After classes, she decided to call Cathy's mom. They had not seen or heard from her, either. Cathy's mom told Ellen they were packing some bags as they talked.

"We're coming up there, Ellen. We'll be there by dark, hopefully."

That afternoon, the local police found Cathy's car. The door was open, but the battery had long since died. There was no sign of an accident. No skid marks or paint streaks from another car. There was no fur or meat or blood on the fender that would have led them to believe she'd hit a deer.

"Gone without a trace," Ellen heard an officer say. Ellen hugged herself as she thought of the terrible things that might have happened to her friend.

Maybe she'd had car trouble and got out to walk and stumbled out into the night, not knowing what to do. It was too cold to stay put, too cold to walk. There were no visible footprints or other car tracks, but it had rained the night before, melting snow and washing away any clues that might have helped determine what had happened.

Ellen talked with several kids on her own. She learned that the boy Cathy had left the game with had been too fresh. He'd gotten mad at her when she'd said no and left her. A couple of students remembered seeing her crying and walking back toward Bushmere.

What were you doing out here, Cathy? Why did you leave campus on a Saturday night?

Cathy's frantic parents had arrived late Monday evening. No one knew where Cathy was or what had happened and she still hadn't been heard from.

By Friday, the police were considering the notion that Cathy had decided to run away, only none of her clothes or possessions were missing except for two things—her cosmetic bag and a pair of pants. Ellen and Cathy had shared a closet and small space long enough for her to know what was missing.

Ellen called home, in tears. Betsy trembled with fear and anxiety during the whole conversation.

"I'm coming home, mom. Maybe Cathy will call me there."

"Honey, why don't you let your father and me drive up and get you. I'd feel so much better that way."

"Mom, I don't think that's necessary. I'll be fine just to drive home. I just don't want to be around here this weekend."

"Ellen, you be careful. No stops. Pee in your pants if you must. Don't stop anywhere. Drive safely and keep your doors locked."

"I will, mom. I promise."

Ellen knew all these things. She had also taken a self - defense refresher as an elective this semester. She was confident as she loaded her car and pulled out of the Maxwell main entrance.

Peter had offered to go with her, but he couldn't follow her. He relied on buses and cabs to get him where he needed to go.

"Thank you, Peter. I really do appreciate the offer. But I'm not sure that would be a good idea just yet. Give me time to tell mom and dad about you. Maybe you can join me for spring break this year?"

Peter smiled that gorgeous smile of his and held her in his arms. He handed her a small card with his name and number on it.

"That's the Cordon Hall commons area phone number. I'll be in there until I get the call from you that you're home safe and sound. If you don't call by, let's say three o'clock, I'm sending the cavalry out to find you."

Ellen glanced at his watch and saw that it was just eleven. "That gives me plenty of time. And I don't plan to stop anywhere."

Peter hugged her again and then watched as she left school. He turned and headed back to Cordon Hall to wait for her call. Freddy pulled out just behind Ellen.

Freddy had no intention of taking Ellen this trip. But he and Lori had sat up late every night this week, planning. And just as Lori had said she would, Ellen headed home for the weekend.

He stayed about five or six car lengths behind her the whole way. It was very quiet inside his old Impala. But in Ellen's Caprice Classic, the music blasted away. She couldn't drive without it going. And when too many commercials started, she'd turn the dial down until it clicked off. Then she would sing her own jams.

At two o'clock, she pulled into Oakdale. She had never been so relieved to be home before in her life. Betsy and Harold came out to hug her when she came to a stop in the drive and tooted the horn. Betsy just held her daughter close for several minutes and Ellen let her. She was so glad to be home.

Freddy slowly pulled on farther down the street. He'd driven exactly two hundred, twenty-two point three miles out of his way. But it was worth it.

Now he knew the route she took, the street name and the town she lived in. The Kelly's had already gone inside when he turned around a half mile down the street and rode past her house again. She never even knew she was being followed.

"Has she called here?" Ellen asked as they made their way into the den.

Betsy shook her head. "Ellen, I'm sure she's fine. They'll find her. The police will bring her home safely."

Ellen hoped for that outcome, but it didn't feel right. There was something about this that was wrong on so many levels. "In my self-defense classes, I've learned to always trust your instincts. If you feel uncomfortable, leave. But mom, my instincts are telling me something bad has happened to Cathy." Ellen began to cry as she spoke.

Daniel and Gaige were trying their best to be nice to each other and to Ellen. They were learning that it really was nice to get along. They had begun to whisper late at night in the room they shared. Betsy could hear them laughing and talking. Her heart skipped a beat every time they got along. That was what she'd been praying for. It was finally happening more and more often.

That evening, after dinner, Ellen eased into the whole Peter conversation. Betsy and Harold listened to her describe Peter. He sounded nice enough, but they'd be the judge of that come Easter. He was welcome to come, they told her and Ellen felt a little bit of happiness, despite the present situation.

The weekend went by too fast, but Ellen had to leave for school again. She didn't wait too long on Sunday before she headed back. She agreed with her mom for once. She didn't want to be out past dark. She would be safely back in her dorm by sundown. Hopefully, Cathy would be there waiting for her with a story about some wild and wacky adventure she'd been on. Maybe she'd say she met some European prince who'd swept her off her feet and took her, by private jet of course, on a whirlwind tour of his homeland…

Freddy sat on the floor in the living room. The scrabble board was splayed out in the center and he, Michelle, Lori, and Cathy played the game together. He told them all about Ellen. Cathy was so happy that her friend and roommate would soon join them.

Peter was waiting outside Bushmere Hall when Ellen pulled in. He gave a quick wave and headed to her car. When she stood, he hugged her briefly and then gave her a very long and passionate kiss. They didn't speak, just continued to hold each other. Peter helped her unload her bags and when they walked up the stairs to her dorm, no one seemed to notice or care that he was there.

When they were inside, Ellen looked to Cathy's bed. Nothing had changed. She was still gone. When Peter saw the tears in her eyes, he comforted her with a smooth and sexy voice. "She'll come home, Ellen. Sooner or later, she'll get tired of whatever she's doing and she'll come home."

Ellen only smiled a little crooked smile and nodded. She sat on the edge of the bed and Peter sat down beside her. He held on to her, not wanting to leave, but knowing he had to. She assured him she was fine as she walked back down to the front foyer with him. She stood inside and shivered when Peter opened the big, glass door. She waved to him and watched until he was out of sight.

Ellen curled up in a ball under her blankets and shook because of the cold. She imagined Cathy in the bed next to her, talking and laughing. It had been exactly one week since she went missing and Ellen was lost without her. She felt a pang of self-pity as she cried herself to sleep. It wasn't like her to feel sorry for herself, but she did. She was lonesome and missed her best friend.

Chapter Twenty-Six

"Detective Leland," Mark said as he answered the heavy phone on his desk.

When it rang, it had caused him to jump a little. The office had been quiet for too long. Resources had grown thin and other detectives' had given up on finding the kidnapper. Leland himself had packed up most of the pictures and files of the girls he had desperately tried to find. The only thing that kept the case fresh in his mind was a promise he'd made to Trish Colbert's family and the mother of Rebecca Lewis. Even though Mrs. Lewis had died, he aimed to keep his word to honor her memory. Occasionally, he and Celeste would have lunch together and discuss the cases. They were working against hope to bring the perp to justice.

"Hello, Detective. This is Officer Terry Wayne. I'm calling you from Maxton County."

Leland wondered what this policeman wanted, but listened as Wayne continued.

"We've had a missing persons report filed up here and I couldn't help but think of the cases you've been working. Seems this young lady just vanished into thin air. I've read about your work down there in Anson and thought we might could discuss a few things."

Leland felt his heart beating harder at the thought that maybe this detective could help bring a killer to justice. "I'm listening, boss. What have you got?"

Terry Wayne continued on. "Cathy Mills, age nineteen. She's a student at Maxwell University. Her roommate reported her missing when she didn't return after a ball game back last month. We have absolutely nothing. No trace of her at all."

Leland wasn't sure what to say. He'd been on this same track for so long. "Is there anything more? Anything at all that could make this easy?"

Wayne sighed. "I wish, detective."

"It sounds all too familiar. What about the roommate? Has she seen anything, heard from Mills at all or does she have a clue where she could be?"

Wayne closed his eyes and pinched the bridge of his nose. He'd asked Ellen Kelly and every other kid that knew her the same things.

"Right now, all we have is an empty car on the side of the road and a roommate beside herself with worry, not to mention the girl's parents, Mr. and Mrs. Mills."

Leland knew the feeling. He rummaged through the boxes of files stacked in the corner of his office and found what he was looking for. He began to tell detective Terry Wayne about all the missing women from Anson and surrounding counties.

"Sounds like you at least smoked him out of your area. But now, if it's the same person, he's moved up here with us. Reckon he moved?"

Leland had considered that and the possibility that he had died. There had been a long gap between girls. It could even be a copycat. He wasn't sure what to tell Wayne.

Between Leland's and Wayne's notes, they had even considered the possibility that the perpetrator was already behind bars on other charges. So many ideas and so little to actually go on.

The phone call lasted another fifty minutes before the two officers decided to meet up and compare notes. When Leland looked out across the almost empty room, he saw Celeste and called for her.

"You up to a little road trip, Celeste?"

"Well, where are you taking me, Mister?"

Mark smiled. He and Celeste had grown close over the last several months. They each wanted to bring Trish's killer to justice. It was nice having a platonic friend to confide in.

Two hours later, the detective and Celeste were on their way to Maxton County. The trunk and the backseat were loaded down with case files and records that they'd kept. The two of them felt some hope glimmering as they made their way North.

Chapter Twenty-Seven

February 17, 1978

By the end of the third week, Ellen had gone to housing and was given a few empty boxes. That afternoon, Cathy's parents arrived to collect her belongings.

Cathy's mom, Colleen, hugged Ellen. Not many words were spoken, just a solemn remembrance that Cathy probably was gone forever. There were no new leads, and no clues to go on. The officer at the scene where Cathy's car had been found was right. She really was gone without a trace.

Peter and Ellen were spending every minute of every weekday together that they could. Ellen went home every weekend. Peter was excited about Easter coming up so he could finally have her all week with no classes or tragedies to interrupt.

Freddy continued to follow her home, following far enough behind to never be spotted. He was learning her habits, where she chose to stop for lunch and bathroom breaks.

Ellen was very predictable. Freddy liked that, as it would make things easier for him when the time came. He liked the way Peter left at the end of each night and the way their kisses were short and sweet. Nothing sloppy or vulgar. Freddy was proud of Ellen for keeping herself pure and clean. She was going to make a perfect addition to his growing family.

On Friday, Ellen packed up, said goodbye to Peter as she always did and pulled out of the parking lot.

So reliable you are, Ellen Kelly.

Ellen turned the dial of the radio, found a station that usually played her favorites, and lit a Marlboro. She began thumping her fingers on the steering wheel as the song blasted out.

You're the one that I want, ooh, ooh, ooh, the one I need, Oh, yes indeed

When that song ended, *Stayin Alive* began. Ellen was as carefree as she'd been in weeks, finally feeling a little better. Ellen had learned that after the jerk at the game got too fresh, Cathy had jumped in her car and headed home on a whim. She'd probably met someone else on the road and was having the time of her life.

So many thoughts raced through Ellen's mind, though. Why was her car on the side of the road? Cathy would not have left the car door open. She worried that Cathy had headed home with no one else to talk to. Ellen had really struggled with that. If she hadn't been so in to Peter, she would have been with Cathy that night. Cathy would never have left. She and Cathy would probably be a party right now, laughing it up and living on the edge. Well, what Ellen considered the edge, anyway. Truly, Cathy knew that better than anyone and hopefully was proving that now.

One hundred miles into her trip home, she had to pull over at a Handy Pantry for gas. While the gas flowed, she ran in to grab a few snacks and a soda.

She waited in line behind a man buying beer. He had to search for change, and then dropped several loose coins. After counting out two dollars in dimes, nickels and pennies, he made small talk with the cashier for what seemed like forever. What should have been a five-minute stop had turned into a twenty-minute luxury break.

Her timing was impeccable. Freddy had just enough time to step out of the dark and puncture one of Ellen's rear tires with a small ice pick. Not too big a hole, just enough to allow air to escape slowly. By the time she got back into the Caprice, Freddy had pulled out and was a few minutes ahead of her. He carefully turned on to a side road, flipped off his lights and patiently waited for Ellen to round the curve.

Just as he was starting to worry that something else had happened, Ellen sped by. Freddy blew out a breath of relief. All he needed now was for another Trish moment to ruin his precise plan.

Moments later, Freddy was in behind her by two car lengths. The road ahead was lonesome and bare. Lori would be as excited as he told her of this adventure. The way he'd planned everything to a scientific tee was exact and calculating. When he saw the Caprice put on brake lights, he smiled to himself.

First, he checked ahead for oncoming traffic. Then he checked the review mirror for cars dragging up the rear. Next, he examined his reflection. He had grown somewhat cocky over the last year, watching his dark hair grow a little each day, trimming those sideburns to be a super spectacle. That's what Lori had called them. Freddy had to agree. He was looking rather good these days. Those scrawny and awkward teen years were way behind him now. Everyone who saw him in town reminded him of that fact.

Freddy put on a turn signal and pulled over just ahead of Ellen. Ellen saw him walking toward her, and she immediately checked to see that the doors were locked.

"Hi there! Car trouble?"

"I don't know for sure. I think it's my tire."

"Let me take a look for you."

Ellen felt a little relief that this nice man was willing to help her. Maybe he'd change her flat for her.

"Yep. She's flat. Gotta spare?"

"Yes, in the trunk."

"Keys?" Freddy smiled. "Don't worry, you can slip them through a crack and never have to get out."

Ellen blew out a whoosh of air and Freddy knew she meant it as a thank you. She pulled the keys out of the ignition, rolled her window down just enough to pass the key to him and quickly rolled it back up.

Freddy walked behind the car and turned the key until the trunk popped open. He already knew there was no spare. He was the one who had taken it out the night before. He walked back around to the driver's side and knelt down beside the door.

"I hate to tell you this, ma'am, but there is no spare back there."

"What? I was sure my dad told me there was one."

"Well, if there was, it ain't there now."

Ellen sat still and quite. She was brainstorming, he could tell.

"I know how you must feel. I have a sister and a mom at home and I would hate to know this was happening to them."

Ellen looked up, buying his attempt at remorse. "Really? What's your sister's name?" Lori had heard that asking a question on the spur of the moment could trick an attacker. She could hear her self-defense instructor's voice in her head clear as day. *"Ask a random question and watch his face. You can usually read in his expression if he's truthful. And if he stumbles around before responding, leave the area immediately."*

"Lori."

"What?"

Freddy gave a small laugh. "You asked me my sister's name. It's Lori."

"Oh, yeah. Sorry. I was lost in thought for a minute."

"I can tell." Look, I don't have a spare either. You can sit here in the freezing cold if you want to. But I'm headed home to Oakdale. I know, I know. You've never heard of it. It's a small town."

Ellen stopped him. "Are you kidding me? I live in Oakdale!"

"No way! Seriously?"

"Yes, way! I do. It is a small town. I grew up there."

"Well, I'm heading there now. I was going to say I could go home, get a spare and come back, but I really don't like the idea of you sitting here alone in the dark. If you'll trust me, I'll take you all the way home. You and your dad can come back tomorrow with a spare. Your car should be fine here overnight.""

Ellen looked directly into Freddy's eyes. They were very innocent and sweet looking. When he gave a little smile toward her, she smiled back.

"Well, I don't have much choice, do I? I have some bags in the trunk. Could you help me with them?"

"Sure. You must be headed home from college for the weekend, too."

"I attend Maxwell."

"Oh, this is too much! I go to Maxwell! I commute, though. My class is late in the afternoons. I hate that!"

"I guess so. What's your major?"

"I don't think I'll tell you."

"Why not? Come on!" Ellen laughed.

With the last bag in the trunk, Freddy told her he'd be right back. He wanted to make sure her doors were secure and the engine was off. What he was really doing was covering his tracks made in the snow along the edge of the road.

How nice! He seems really concerned about me. What a relief! Ellen was thankful that this young man had crossed her path tonight. Freddy jumped in, a little too eager to help. *Calm down, Freddy,* he thought to himself. He started the motor and pulled out onto the dark road.

"So? Tell me. I won't laugh, I promise."

"I'm a mortician. I'm taking an extra class now, gerontology."

"Fantastic! I really mean that. That's like, really far out, man!"

Freddy smiled as he checked her expression. She was being honest.

"Thanks. My dad ran a funeral home growing up. I found it interesting and decided to do it myself. I'm new in Oakdale and I hope to open a funeral home there in the future. Well, if I ever pass this class."

Ellen listened intently. She shared with him all about Cathy's disappearance, how hard trig was and how she'd met Peter.

"I know him!" Freddy gasped. "I've seen him around campus a lot this semester."

"Wow! Small world, huh?"

"Yes, it is. I'm sorry about your friend, Kelly."

"Cathy. Her name is Cathy, not Kelly."

"Sorry, I guess I wasn't paying attention. So what does campus security think? Any ideas from the local cops?"

"Nothing. It's like she just vanished without a trace. They found her car and talked with people that saw her on campus earlier that day, but nothing else. No clues at all."

Ellen looked out the window and noticed that the snow had started falling again.

"I hate driving in the snow," Freddy commented.

"Me, too. I'm kinda glad I had a flat. I don't feel safe driving in dangerous conditions. I was a little lonely, too and feeling sorry for myself. I miss Cathy."

"I'm sure you do, Ellen. I'm sure you do."

When they reached exit 4A to Oakdale, Freddy continued on.

"Uh, oh. You missed our turn."

"Actually, Ellen, I've got a bigger night planned. But don't worry, you'll be fine. You'll love what I have in store!"

Ellen could feel herself sinking. *What have I got myself into?* "Actually, I just want to go home, thanks."

Freddy laughed that eerie laugh of his. "Oh, that's what they all say. You should have heard Cathy!"

"What? Cathy? You've seen her?"

"She's at my house right now, babe!"

"Oh, thank God! And she's okay?"

"Sure she is. She's far out, you know?"

Ellen smiled. "Yeah, she is."

Chapter Twenty-Eight

It wasn't until Ellen realized how far they had traveled that she started to feel apprehensive. "How did you and Cathy meet?"

"She was on the road, and stopped to help me. I was exhausted after a long day at school, you know? Thought I'd pull off and nap when there she was! Knocking on my window and asking if I was okay. A very thoughtful girl."

"So, she just got in with you?"

"Well, it took a little persuading. But she was glad once we got home. I have other girls, too. Lori calls them her sisters because we're all one big happy family, you know? Safe and sound and happy."

Ellen was looking out the window.

"So, how much farther? You said you lived in Oakdale. Where are we?"

"Only a little farther, babe. Not too much longer."

Ellen sank down in the imitation leather. She could feel the sweat popping out all over her anxious body.

"So she just left her car by the side of the road and didn't call anyone? That's not the Cathy I know. No, something's wrong here."

"Don't worry, babe. I'm telling you, Cathy is super!"

Freddy smiled at Ellen, but now his smile looked deviant. He had completely lost the innocent look and Ellen's instincts were growing wilder by the second.

"Look. I don't want any trouble. Just drop me off at the next town. I'm not interested in going further. Thanks, but I'll be fine. I'll call my dad and he'll pick me up. An all-night diner or even gas station will be fine."

"Oh, aren't you just the polite little girl all of a sudden. Sweet and innocent, huh?"

Ellen looked at Freddy puzzled. "What?"

"I know what you and Peter do up in that empty dorm room, Ellen. He stays until the wee hours of the morning. You disgust me. You and Peter both. You really should be ashamed."

"How do you—wait. You've been spying on me?"

"No! Not spying, Ellen. Watching. Waiting."

"Waiting? For what?"

"For the perfect moment to make you mine."

Ellen's adrenaline kicked in to overdrive. Her mind was racing. She was trying desperately to remember all the things she'd learned in her self-defense courses. She'd actually taken two classes back in Oakdale. One was a beginner's class; the second was a refresher course. Then at Maxwell, she had taken kickboxing her freshman year, along with self-defense for advanced learners. This year, she was actually helping teach the class as a volunteer. She gained an extra credit and received volunteer credit, something she needed on her resume.

All those classes and all that learning were no more than a blank canvas in her mind right now. She was trying to think, but her head was foggy and she felt panic boiling just underneath the surface. *Think, Ellen. Think. What should I do? What do I say right now to turn this around?* And that's when it hit her.

"So, what was Cathy wearing when you picked her up?"

"Ah, a white blouse that was almost see-through. Dark blue jeans, white boots, and a crimson coat. Her scarf was white, to match her blouse."

Ellen was confused. This technique was supposed to catch the predator off guard, but he'd described her outfit to a tee. So, that meant he really did have Cathy.

"What's she been doing all this time?"

"A little of this, a lot of that." Freddy winked at Ellen.

"What? What's *that*?"

"You know what I mean, babe. The same thing you've been doing with Peter on those long, lonesome nights."

"But Peter and I haven't, well, *done* it."

Freddy slowed down and looked at her.

"Honest? You haven't spoiled yourself with that geek?"

"Peter is not a geek! But, no, I haven't. I want to wait 'till I know for sure. You know, I want to know it's true love. Maybe even marriage."

"Oh, that's beautiful, Ellen. I'm so proud of you. Really. I'm very proud. It makes me feel honored that your first time will be with me."

With that, Ellen pulled up on the door handle. Anything was better than this. What was the worst that could happen? A few broken bones? A slight concussion?

"Whoa!" Freddy slammed on the brakes and as Ellen leaped from the car, he reached to grab her. His hand waved wildly towards her, but she toppled out onto the snowy ground.

"What the hell do you think you're doing, Ellen Kelly?"

Ellen hit the ground hard and began to roll uncontrollably down the embankment.

Freddy pulled off onto the shoulder, pushed the gear shifter up to park and stumbled out of the driver's seat. He'd never had this happen before. But then again, he usually drugged his victims. He had enjoyed the conversation with Ellen and really didn't want to inject her.

I left the vial in the console! Freddy screamed in his mind.

Right now, he didn't care. He had to catch Ellen. He ran hard and fast. His legs were burning from the exertion. Maybe that meant Ellen's legs were burning, too. Maybe that meant she was out of breath and slowing down.

The night was dark and with no streetlights, searching her out was a difficult task. He ran quickly in the direction she had taken, but she was gone, nowhere in sight.

"Damn you, Ellen! Damn you!" he yelled out into the cold night. He wondered if Ellen could hear him. She couldn't be far.

Ellen was running like she'd never run before. Her legs felt as if they had a million ants crawling up them, stinging and biting her as they scurried. She was trying to keep calm, but when she heard him yell out, she knew he was closer than she'd thought.

The night around her was too quiet. There were no cars, no sounds, nothing. She stopped momentarily to survey her surroundings. She was in a field. Probably a cornfield during the summer months, but right now it was as barren as everything else around her. There could be a row of trees to the rear of the field, but she couldn't tell what was ahead of her.

She continued running, hoping for something she could hide behind, under, or atop. This field had to end sooner or later. It couldn't go on forever.

A cramp in her thigh brought her down. She fell face first into the muddy snow. As she pushed herself up, she heard his footsteps nearing her. She willed herself up and started to run again. She fought through the pain she felt. Ellen honestly thought her lungs would burst. But even if they did, at least she'd die from that and not at this maniac's hands. He would not rape her. She was determined that that wouldn't happen, no matter what.

It may have been an old corn stalk, maybe a rock. Ellen didn't see what caused her to trip, but here she was, lying in the mud again. Before she could rise to her knees, she felt a hand grab her long ponytail.

"Gotcha!" That was all Freddy could get to escape from his mouth. He held on to her with an iron grip as he lifted her up.

The pain on her scalp was even worse than what she felt in her lungs and in her legs. Freddy never eased up, not one bit.

By the time they had made their way to the car, Ellen was a little better. She pushed her knee up and into Freddy's abdomen. She was aiming lower, but this would work. He let go of her and hugged his stomach and she was running again, this time down the road. Surely a car would see her soon. There had to be a trucker or someone.

But Freddy was stronger than she gave him credit for. He rushed forward and pushed her down on the pavement. Her face began to burn in pain from the cuts the pavement made.

"Oh, no. Ellen, look what you made me do. Now you won't look your best for Lori. She'll be disappointed. You've been naughty. And now you'll pay for it."

"Please, don't. No! No!" Ellen screamed out. She was fighting as hard as she could against the weight of this man.

"What? You think I'll rape you?"

"You said you were!"

Freddy smiled and shook his head. "I don't think it's called rape when my girls are begging me for it."

Freddy led her to the car, even though she was kicking, screaming, trying to grab hair, anything to avoid that car.

"You'll see. I'll show you. I'll let you watch Lori and me. And soon, you'll participate. But not right away. No, I have to prepare you first."

"I don't want to watch. I want to go home."

"It's funny. That's what they all say, but in the end, you'll want it. You'll want me and you'll want Cathy, too."

"That's disgusting. I would never want sex with Cathy." Ellen was repulsed by the notion.

"You won't have a choice. Now, you must be good from here on out, Ellen. We have a long drive ahead of us and I won't stand for more trouble."

Ellen muttered something under her breath, but Freddy didn't care to know what she'd said. It just didn't matter.

She had so many things going through her mind. When she began to cry loudly, Freddy looked at her and rolled his eyes.

"Really? Do you insist on screaming? It's very unbecoming of a lady, Ellen."

"Let me go, you, you sick twisted—"

"What? What do you really want to call me, Ellen? You think you're so perfect. So sweet and clean and perfect? Well, you're not. Not like Lori. No one could ever be like Lori to me and there is nothing, I mean nothing perverse or sick or twisted about that!" Now Freddy was screaming.

He could feel his teeth grinding together, something he hadn't done in years. He reached over and began to fumble around in the console. When his fingers touched the vial, he grabbed at it and pulled it out. "I had looked forward to this drive with you, Ellen. It was supposed to give me the chance to know you better. I like to tell Lori all about the friends I bring her. I had hoped you could keep me company, too. But you're screwing up my plan and I can't have that. Sorry."

As he talked, Ellen saw the syringe coming at her. She moved as close to the door as she could and fumbled with the door, looking for the handle again. But she was too frightened to look away from the needle. She found the knob and was pulling it up when the needle plunged deep into her neck. She gave a small little whimper and her hand dropped from the door. She stared up at Freddy and within three seconds, her eyes closed.

Freddy was glad he'd taken the time to tweak the amount of detrepanol he injected into Ellen. This new amount was much better at subduing the girls.

"Little high and mighty bitch. You though you could get away from me, didn't you? Well, I showed you. I showed them all."

Ellen could hear him talking, but she couldn't force herself to speak. She desperately tried to move, to open her eyes, but nothing happened. As Freddy rambled on, his voice became distant and soon she was sound asleep. She had only been asleep for a few minutes when her first dream began. She and Cathy were walking around on campus and Cathy began to laugh.

"What? What's so funny, kiddo?"

"Oh, nothing. I was just thinking that we come from different families and from different parts of the country. We didn't even know each other until fall semester began. I had never heard of Ellen Kelly."

"Same here. I didn't know you from Adam."

"Yeah, I know. And now look, Ellen. We were taken by the same person and killed the same way."

The dream ended and Ellen was in a white fog, but still couldn't move or speak. She tried so hard to wake, but she couldn't do it. Then a foggy scene appeared and she was dreaming again. She could see something in the distance. Her body slowly moved forward, toward the object in her dream. She wasn't walking, but floating.

Soon, she could make out a box. She was drifting closer and closer to the box and eventually could tell that it wasn't a box at all. It was a headstone. The letters were faded and old. All she could make out was an E, an L, and a Y. As she struggled to focus on the letters, she heard someone speak. She turned to see two young girls, maybe sixteen or so.

"Do you know what happened to her?"

"Yeah, I heard my grandmother talking about her."

"Back in the '70s, a madman murdered a bunch of girls about our age. She was one of them." The girl talking pointed a slender finger toward the stone. Ellen turned from the girls to see the tombstone was clearer now. It read:

Ellen Kelly

September 22, 1959- February 17, 1978

Gone but never forgotten

Daughter, sister, friend

Ellen jerked awake from her nightmare. She realized too late that she was about to enter a new one. She was strapped down to a metal table and Freddy was standing over her.

Chapter Twenty-Nine

Betsy walked across the living room floor back and forth. Her pacing was taking Harold's annoyance to a whole new level.

"She's fine, Bet. She'll be home soon. You know how it goes out on the open road. Could be construction, a traffic jam, anything."

"I know that Harold. That's why I'm worried. She could be the one causing the jam. She could be in a ten-car pileup right now for all we know. She could be in a ditch. And don't give me that construction bit, either. On a Friday night? No, that wouldn't be it. I don't care what kind of job you have."

Betsy was referring to Harold's career. He'd worked construction for years. It was actually supposed to be a part time summer job after he'd graduated but he'd ended up making a career of it instead. When the summer ended, other teens moved on to college, but he'd stayed with the company. He'd surprised himself and disappointed his parents. For three years he'd talked of college, a business degree and joining his father at his coffee cup factory.

A career in coffee cups sounded lame after a whole summer with the most adventurous men he'd ever talked to. So, he made construction a professional career, eventually finding a corporate ladder even there. Three years after the heat of the summer, the freezing cold of winter and the pollen infested springs, he'd applied for a foreman position. He must have been good at what he did, because he'd gotten the job. He was so excited when he was handed a white hard hat and retired the yellow one. By the end of that year, he was wearing a green one.

Twenty years later, he owned the company. Kelly Construction had done well through the years and put a roof over his head and food on his table. He took care of his children and wife and now, looking back, he realized that even his parents had grown proud of him.

"Betsy, I promise. Any minute now, Ellen will drive up, toot the horn and expect her brothers and me to go out and unload her suitcases."

Betsy hoped he was right, but she had a feeling gnawing in the pit of her stomach she'd never had before. Something was wrong. She could just feel it. She looked up to the old cuckoo clock in the hallway again. Only two minutes had passed since she last checked. Eleven o'clock, and still no Ellen. Midnight came and went, and still no Ellen.

At one A.M., she dialed the Oakdale Police Department. By now, Harold was as worried as she was.

"Oakdale Police Department," the woman on the other end answered.

"Yes, my name is Elizabeth Kelly. My daughter, Ellen hasn't come home yet and I'm worried sick."

"Okay, ma'am. How old is your daughter?"

"Nineteen. And she is heading home from—"

"She is nineteen? How long has she been missing?"

"She was supposed to home by now. She was driving home from Maxwell University. She's always home by now."

"So, technically, she isn't missing," the woman bluntly stated.

"Well, technically, I don't suppose—"

Once again, the woman interrupted. "Mrs. Kelly, when your daughter has been missing for twenty-four hours, call back. She could be out with friends. Maybe at a bar getting hit on. She's nineteen and she's a college kid."

"But Ellen's not like that." Betsy was really annoyed at the response she was getting.

"Oh, no ma'am. I'm sure your daughter isn't like the millions of girls in colleges all over the country. Your daughter isn't one to go to parties or flirt with the boys."

"She really isn't. I'm telling you, something's wrong."

The rude operator hung up before Betsy could comment further. The woman, Dianne, shook her head. "It's never like their daughter, is it?"

Braden, the other officer on duty laughed. "Oh, no. Never *their* daughter. *Their* daughter doesn't get high and party hard. *Their* daughter's don't hook up with the boys and get lucky." Braden sank his teeth into another brownie. "I swear, Dianne, you make the best brownies ever."

Dianne smiled. "Well, thank you, sir."

Just then the phone rang again. Dianne answered with the same bland voice she'd used with Betsy.

"Oakdale Police Department, can I help you?"

Harold's voice on the other end caught Dianne off guard.

"My name is Harold Kelly. And if you hang up on me like you just did to my wife, I'll call the captain myself and report your sorry ass. Our daughter is not out partying. I understand that plenty of college kids do, but ours isn't one of them. She always arrives on time. She's a very mature and considerate young woman. Her roommate disappeared last month and she's been coming home every weekend since. She would never have us worry like this for no reason. Now, what can we do?" Harold seldom got mad, but he could feel himself shaking all over with anger.

"I apologize, sir. It's just that we are getting calls like crazy lately every time a young girl is late arriving home or to work or school."

Harold set back in his recliner and took in a deep breath. Betsy stood over him with her hands up in the air. She wanted to know what the impolite woman was saying.

"Until your daughter has been missing for twenty-four hours, there isn't anything we can do."

"Can you send someone out to Highway 74 and just make sure she's not stranded somewhere? She takes that same road home every Friday. She could have been in an accident. The roads up that way are still slick at night and early mornings."

Dianne rolled her eyes at Braden. "Sure thing, Mr. Kelly. I'll dispatch an officer in Tridell County to take a gander up that way."

"Thank you. Here's our number." Harold called out their phone number, and then thanked the woman again.

"Well? What did she say?"

"They're sending out a cruiser to check the area. They'll call us back soon."

"Maybe we should head out that way, too. Gaige and Daniel could stay here in case she comes home while we're out."

"Yeah, dad," Gaige chimed in.

"Sure thing. We could stay up and wait on her," Daniel added.

"Let's give it until the cops call back first. If they don't see anything, we'll head out," Harold replied.

Betsy nodded her head in agreement. It was a very long drive and could take longer in the icy conditions. She began pacing again and Daniel and Gaige sat quietly watching the clock. Harold stood and stretched, and then grabbed Betsy and she broke down. This was the first time Daniel and Gaige had seen their mother cry. When she started to really sob, they knew this was bad.

Daniel thought back to last weekend when he and Ellen had fought.

"I'm telling mom about the smoke butts out back, sister, dear."

"Daniel, grow up already. Don't tell. Please?"

"Five dollars." Daniel held out his hand. As soon as the money was placed in his palm, he grinned and ran downstairs to where Betsy stood at the oven.

"Mom?" Daniel said, getting her attention.

"What is it, Daniel?"

"I'm worried about Ellen."

"What on earth for, son?"

"She smokes. I've got proof."

Ellen walked into the kitchen just in time to hear the little brat tattle.

"You butt hole!" Ellen yelled.

Daniel turned around to see his sister seething. "What? Smoking causes cancer. Didn't they teach you that yet at Maxwell?"

Betsy cut through the argument. "I already know, dear. Gaige beat you to it."

Ellen groaned. She had given him a five to stay quiet, too.

As Ellen and Daniel continued to fight, Betsy sent them both out of the room. She looked at Ellen and said, "We'll talk about this later, young lady."

And Ellen knew they would. She knew this was just one more thing for her mom to nag about. She didn't dare roll her eyes at her mother that time. She quietly stepped out into the living room and caught Daniel by the loop in his jeans. She bent down low to him and whispered. "We'll talk about this later, young lady."

She was calling him a lady and that made Daniel even madder. "I'm telling!" he shouted. Ellen just laughed and started up the stairs. She looked back down to him and held up one middle finger his way.

"Mom! Ellen just gave me the bird!" he whined. Ellen laughed loudly as she trotted to her room, slamming the door behind her.

Now, he just wanted his sister home, safe and sound. He swore under his breath that he'd never, ever be mean to Ellen again. He promised himself that he'd be good to her from then on if God would just send her home safely.

Gaige was thinking about Ellen, too. His mind drifted back to last summer when he'd found her diary.

She had written about liking Thom Howard from biology. She had decided that she wanted him to be her first. He wasn't too sure what that meant until he flipped the page three entries over. He learned all about how Susan Cowl had lost her virginity in the back of Ted Brewer's Mustang. His sister must be a slut cause she had written the word *sex*. She had written all about her bra being too tight and how mom had promised her a trip to Dolson's Department Store before going off to college that fall.

Gaige had read so many entries in that book, each one more thrilling than the last. He was almost to the part where Ellen told about having her *period*. How her menstrual cramps kept her out of gym class every month. He was just getting ready to call Edwin, his best friend, and ask him what some of the words meant when Ellen walked in.

"Oh, no you didn't!" she screamed at him.

Gaige backed up trying to ease out of the room when Ellen caught him.

"Don't hurt me!" he yelled. "Or I'll tell mom you want to lose it with Thom Howard!"

Ellen let him go and stood there shocked. Did he even know what that meant? She had written her heart out on those pages and now her dumb brother knew each secret.

She didn't speak to him for a week until finally she got even. She bribed Daniel for some secrets of her own. Finally, during dinner one night, Ellen got her revenge.

"So, Gaige. I understand you got an A in math last time. That's great."

Gaige's mouth hung open, revealing a half-eaten meatball. "Yeah, thanks." He could feel the bomb dropping, but didn't know how to stop it.

"Mom, you should be so proud of your little boy. I'd call his teacher. I'd want to know how on earth he could bring that F up to an A in one six weeks session."

Gaige felt a knot forming in his gut. The only thing he could do to change the subject was to knock over a glass of tea. The commotion did exactly what he'd wanted. As Betsy hurried to get a towel, Ellen used two fingers to point to her own eyes, and then turned them to Gaige. *I'm watching you,* was the suggestion she made.

By the time the tea was wiped up, the conversation had moved on to something else entirely. But Gaige never rambled around in Ellen's room again. He had learned his lesson. The last thing he wanted was for his mother to find out he'd changed his own grade in Mrs. Tyler's grade book. The old hag of a teacher never noticed, but his mom would.

He missed his sister now. He wondered where she was, what she was doing, and if she ever did lose it with Thom. He just wanted her here now.

When the old clock struck two, the little cuckoo bird stuck out his head and began to sing. The sound jarred all four of the Kelly's.

"Okay, Betsy. Let's go. Get dressed and we're heading out toward Maxwell."

Betsy looked down in confusion until she realized she was wearing her nightgown. "What about the boys, Harold? We can't leave them here at this hour."

Harold thought for a second, and then said, "I'll call Jackson. He and his wife can come over. He owes me one, anyway."

Betsy shook her head and hurried to her room to change while Harold called Jackson, one of the foremen at Kelly Construction. Thirty minutes later, Jackson and Mary arrived. Betsy hugged each of her boys and gave some simple instructions to Mary while Harold warmed the car. When he honked the horn, she said, "Okay, well, boys, be good and don't give Mrs. Mary any trouble. Try to sleep some. We'll call you when we can." She ran out to meet Harold. Daniel and Gaige waved goodbye as they watched them roll out of sight.

Mary and Jackson tried to make things fun for the boys. They tried to show Mary how to work the joystick for Atari, they were allowed to watch the late, late movie and ate popcorn.

Mary and Jackson were as kind as could be, but it still didn't help. They were as worried as anyone about Ellen.

Chapter Thirty

Ellen was still very groggy. She tried to focus her eyes, but everything was blurry and doubled. She turned her head this way and that, but nothing was making sense.

"Well, you're finally awake!" Freddy sang out. He was standing behind her, watching her every move. She had run twice now, she wouldn't do that again. He'd make sure she stayed right where she belonged—here with him and his girls.

As her memory started coming back, she recognized the voice coming from directly behind her. It belonged to Freddy the freak. She tried to speak, but her mouth had been gagged with something. Her legs and arms felt too heavy. She attempted to move, and then saw that she was tied down. The table under her was cold and hard. The light above her was too bright and made her squint.

She wiggled maybe an inch or so, but Freddy had a good, tight hold on her. She began to work at one of the cuffs on her hand until it was somewhat loose. She wriggled until she could almost slip her wrist through the opening. But she made sure Freddy didn't see that. She lay there as calmly as she could.

"I'm glad you're finally accepting your role, Ellen. It's much better when you don't fight." Freddy held out his hands and stretched his arms up over his head. "Welcome to my workspace, by the way."

Ellen frantically looked around, but her sight was limited because of the leather restraint across her forehead.

Freddy pulled up a stool and sat near enough to her that she could see him well. She could even see the ugly pores along the bridge of his pointed nose. She lay there helplessly staring at him. What else could she do?

"Once upon a time, long, long ago, a young boy named Freddy helped his dad. His dad was Fred, too. But just Fred, you understand? I'm Freddy, he was Fred. Well, Fred ran and operated the only funeral parlor in town. And this, you see, was where he worked to make men look as if they were just sleeping. This is where he made the women look more beautiful in death than they ever had in life."

Ellen blinked as Freddy continued.

"Once, I had a voice I heard all the time. I called it my *inside-voice*. Only I could hear it. It said terrible things, Ellen. Just horrid, putrid things. It was really frightening. But one night, my inside-voice shared a secret with me. You want to know what that secret was, Ellen?"

Ellen could feel the warmth surrounding her inner thighs.

"Oh, poor baby. I'm sorry, Ellen. You've gone and pissed yourself. That's okay. Sometimes the workstation gets a little messy. So you just do what comes natural. Now, where was I? Oh, yes. The inside-voice. Well, the voice told me that I could have any woman I wanted. Any woman, Ellen! Can you believe that? It's true. One day, the local English teacher died. Miss Kate was very sick, but so beautiful. Dreamy, actually. And when dad finished with her, she looked so peaceful, so natural and graceful. At first, I tried to drown out the voice. My inside-voice was telling me I could have Mrs. Kate.

"But, Ellen, Mrs. Kate was *dead.* That night, I snuck out to the building, pulled her out of the drawer, and looked down at her. She was helpless, but needy. And Ellen, I swear, Mrs. Kate opened her eyes and smiled up at me! She did! And she opened her legs and begged me to go inside her. *Begged* me, Ellen. My inside-voice cheered me on while I did her. That was *my* first time. I was only fourteen, but I knew what to do."

Ellen could feel the vomit rising in her throat. She swallowed hard to avoid choking. She breathed in deep, calming breaths. Freddy stood and motioned what he'd done to that poor corpse.

"It was so nice. It was good, Ellen. Mrs. Kate told me it was good and thanked me for taking her. I said *you're very welcome* and placed her back in the drawer, safe and sound. Things continued on like that for a while. But, you know, very few hot chicks die. It can get lonely during those dry spells.

"Now, you may not know this, and I know you'd never believe it, but school wasn't easy for me. Back then, I was all skin and bones and geeky to the max! But, I persevered. Kids were always mean to me. I guess every school has that. Then the most amazing thing happened my senior year. I met Lori. Lori Eades, the most beautiful woman in Anson County. And she liked me, too!"

Ellen was blocking out most of what Freddy said. She tried to think of pleasant things. Her mom, her dad, her brothers. Tears filled her eyes as she thought of them.

Then her mind got stuck on an image of Peter. She couldn't accept that she'd never see her loved ones again. As Freddy went on and on about this Lori girl, she wriggled her left arm slightly. The cuff on it moved some too. Freddy seemed to be in some kind of trance, droning on and on, so she worked diligently to break free.

"The only problem was, Lori died in a terrible car crash. Some idiot hit the car she was in. She was thrown clear through the windshield. That was what killed her. The impact on the glass windshield killed Lori. She was dead before she hit the pavement. I guess if you've got to go, it was the best way. I say that because she landed on her head and skidded a long ways before her body came to a stop. By then, the pavement had seared off most of her hair and taken her ear off completely. It was a sad, sad day for Anson County."

Freddy stood again and looked out through a small window. He remained quiet for a few seconds. Ellen could hear cars passing. They were in town! There was hope for her yet! Then he turned to face her.

"The good thing was that Lori fell in love with me. After she was brought here to be prepared. But that didn't matter to me. I made her pretty again and she was so grateful, she offered herself to me. Lori lost it that night to me. I have always admired her for saving herself for me."

Freddy hit himself in the chest and tears streamed down his face. "We've been madly in love ever since!" Freddy wiped his eyes.

Ellen was starting to pay attention to his words again. She couldn't figure out what she and Cathy had to do with Lori or anyone else for that matter. She would be enlightened soon.

"Well, we buried Lori. It was a hot, humid day. I remember being so nervous and sick with worry. How could I let them bury my sweet Lori? I couldn't, Ellen. I just couldn't."

He walked around to her other side and began tinkering with something she couldn't see. He was still talking as he worked.

"That night, after Lori was in the ground, I heard my inside voice so clearly. It had a plan. A brilliant plan to bring Lori back home."

A loud bang startled Ellen. She craned her neck, but was still too confined to see what this crazy man was doing.

Freddy dropped a razor and bent down to retrieve it. He fell down on the floor and began to sob loudly. These were thoughts he'd kept to himself for a very long time. He didn't like trudging through those terrible memories.

He rocked himself back and forth, back and forth. As he did that, Ellen was working the restraint on her left leg. She was pretty sure if Freddy remained in his thoughts, she could pull herself up.

Freddy held on to the table and pulled himself up. He snorted back snot and continued on. "How could I go on without Lori? So, my inside-voice told me to find her. It wasn't easy, finding the perfect replacement, but I eventually found the one girl that would suffice."

Ellen looked to see Freddy standing there, looking off and in a trance of his own. She used that time to pull hard on her leg. She could feel the skin pulling away, but a raw leg was better than what she feared would happen otherwise.

When the leg broke free, she very gently placed it back where it would be under the strap. Freddy never even noticed.

When he came back to himself, he couldn't remember where he'd been in his conversation with Ellen. He picked up the razor and shook his head. He couldn't recall getting lost like that before. It frightened him.

"Ellen, I apologize. I don't know what came over me. I'm going to remove your gag now. Can you be a good girl for me? If you promise not to scream, I'll go get Lori for you. Okay?"

Ellen moved her head up and down as much as she could.

"Good girl." He slowly pulled the gag down around her neck. He untied the strap around her head so that cutting her hair would be easier. Ellen took in a breath of air and could smell the recognizable odor of antiseptic. It smelled like a doctor's office in here.

"When I realized I couldn't have Lori, my inside voice pointed something out to me. If I couldn't have her, I could make her. Of course, she had to be adjusted somewhat. I had to shave her bald and remove her ear. Then, I had to embalm her, just like Lori. She wasn't very happy with that, but I promise you, Ellen, afterward, she was so thrilled to be here!"

Freddy sighed. "But, my mom and dad were still living here. Lori had to stay locked away in my room all day and night. She told me she was lonely. She needed a friend. That's when I went out and did some shopping. I brought friends home to Lori and that made her ecstatic!"

Freddy began to cut Ellen's hair very methodically. Ellen just lay still and allowed him to do what he wanted to do.

It's only hair, Ellen. It'll grow back. Just stay calm and wait for the right moment.

"So, when can I meet Lori?"

Freddy was relieved that Ellen had finally stopped fighting.

"Soon. Very soon. She is excited to meet you."

He clipped away until her hair was short enough to shave. He took the razor from his work tray and carefully shaved away the last remnants of hair.

"We've got to tidy up that scrape, too."

Ellen had forgotten about her fall on the road. "Yeah, it hurts, Freddy. Thank you for taking care of me."

Freddy patted her bald head and smiled down at her. He looked around and saw that there was nothing to use to fix her cut. He knew he needed to do everything he could now before he began the embalming process.

"Tell you what. I'll run in and try to find some ointment for that. I'll be right back, I promise."

"Okay. Don't be long, Freddy." The smile on Ellen's face warmed his heart.

Freddy trotted away from the building. As his footsteps grew farther away, Ellen got busy. First, she slid both hands out of the leather cuffs. One leg was free already, but she didn't have time to wiggle the other one free. She saw basic buckles on top, near her knee. She unbuckled them quickly and jumped off the table.

She had to run, she had to hide. She looked around, surveying the area. There was only a set of metal drawers on the far end of the room. *No way, Ellen. No way in hell are you getting in there.* There was no good place to go. She hurried to the door and looked out.

She saw the big, white farmhouse not too far away. Down the drive was the main road, but she didn't know how long it would be before another car passed and she didn't want to risk Freddy catching her again.

She slipped out into the dark lawn, her freshly shaved head feeling the fierce cold. She ran across the yard and peered in through the window. There was a woman at the table, her back to Ellen. She tried to get her attention, without making too much noise, but it wasn't enough. The woman didn't hear her.

She could see that other than the one woman, there wasn't anyone else in the kitchen. She tiptoed to the door, and very quietly pulled it open. There was no squeak from the hinges, thank God. She walked around the table and whispered to the woman.

"Help me, please! Freddy is after me. Can you hear me?"

She knelt down to the woman and realized immediately that she was dead. Ellen covered her mouth to prevent a scream from bursting out. Ellen had just met Paula. She could hear steps on the stairs and slipped into the darkness of the next room.

Freddy ran out the door and it slammed shut after him. The door bounced back a few times, clapping against the hinges. Finally, it stopped and Ellen turned the corner. To her horror, she saw another woman sitting on the sofa. She too was dead. Her white eyes stared blankly toward Ellen. She turned quickly to her right to see a third corpse. This was where Freddy had left Lisa and Michelle.

There was another door at the far end of the living room. She hurried to the door. Ellen was in a nightmare. She saw Cathy, lying on the floor with her legs sprawled out in front of her. Lori sat on a chair next to her. She held a magazine on her lap, but there was nothing this poor woman could read.

Around the room, Ellen was spinning. Her head twirled in horror and disgust. From here, she could see what appeared to be a porch. The walls were windows, *a sun porch*. There, she would find Amber. Ellen didn't know what to do. Nothing she'd ever learned in self-defense could have prepared her for a scene as gruesome as this one.

She was jolted from her fixed stare at Amber when the kitchen door slammed shut.

"Lori! Lori! Something awful has happened! Ellen is gone! Have you seen her? Tell me, Lori. Did she come in here?"

Ellen crouched down behind the wicker chair in the sunroom. She was horrified by what she heard next.

"No, baby. I didn't see her. Oh, Freddy, please find her! I want to meet Ellen. She sounds so far out! Please bring her back so I can meet her!"

Freddy's voice was high and deranged.

Oh dear God. He thinks Lori is talking. She is talking, through Freddy.

Ellen wanted so badly to get back to Cathy. But there was nothing she could do for her best friend now. Cathy was dead. Ellen could feel the tears forming in her eyes. All this time, she wanted so badly to believe that Cathy was somewhere safe. But she was stuck here, getting shaved. She was here getting the life drained out of her.

When Ellen heard the door slam again, she rose and walked cautiously back to where Cathy was. She heard Freddy crank up. She had to find a phone and fast. She had to get help.

Freddy sped down the drive. This one was feisty. And in the end, he believed that would make things even better. Lori would appreciate all the trouble he'd gone through for her.

She would love him more than ever. But first, he had to find the little wench who wouldn't sit still.

Chapter Thirty-One

Ellen was panicking, even though she knew that was the number one no-no in self-defense. She wanted to stay with Cathy. She had to phone for help. "I'll come back to you, Cathy, I swear," she said through trembling lips.

She wrapped around the house, realizing that the layout of the rooms literally made a circle from one room to the next. Any other time, she might have actually liked the open floor plan, but at this moment, she was fighting the feeling of being helpless.

She found the kitchen again, and tried not to look at the woman sitting at the table. Her bald head was patchy between a light brown and a fleshy-white color. Ellen could feel the vomit rising up in her throat, so she swallowed hard and turned away. Paula's eyes were fixed on something Ellen couldn't see and she wondered what Paula had seen last.

What horror did you witness before you died?

She saw the old, black phone hanging near the door leading to the sun room. Ellen stumbled across the yellow linoleum until she grabbed the wall for balance. She lifted the receiver and waited for a dial tone. She felt a wash of relief and regained control when the tone buzzed in her ear. She slid her quivering finger in to the "O" hole and pulled upward. When she released the dial, it made a clicking sound all the way back down to its original place. The sound seemed to cut through a silent nightmare, spilling out in front of her.

"Operator. City and state, please," the operator's voice pierced through the line and into her and Ellen cried tears of joy. Her bad dream was finally about to end.

"Oh, thank God! Help me! I'm being held against my will and Freddy is looking for me!"

"City and state, please," the operator repeated.

"Oh, I don't know where I am! Oh, God! I have no idea what town I'm in. It's an old farm house. There's a building beside it. It has a gravel driveway."

"Miss, I'd love to help you, but I need a town or state."

Ellen's tears of joy quickly turned to sorrow. "But I don't know where I am. Please, you have to help me. Please help me. Please."

The operator dialed the FBI hotline number and softly spoke to Ellen.

"I'm putting you through to the Federal Bureau of Investigation. Best of luck."

Her voice was replaced with a ringing sound. Ellen slid down the wall, tears streaming down her face. When a man answered, she didn't know where to start.

"FBI hotline. This is Special Agent Weston. Can I help you? Hello?"

"Please, you have to help me. I'm being held captive in an old house. The man who took me is Freddy, I don't know his last name."

If Ellen did know, she was too upset now to remember that Freddy was Fred Lee Junior.

"He is looking for me. There are other women here, too. They're all dead. There is at least five, no, six women here and they are all dead! One of them is my friend, Cathy. She went missing from school last month and she's here!"

Ellen was trying to remain calm, but all of her emotions washed over her in one sudden flood. She sobbed in between words.

"Where are you, ma'am?" Agent Weston asked.

"I don't know where I am!"

"Okay, calm down. Can you see any road signs from where you are?"

Ellen was stuck on his words, *calm down*. Easy for him to say. He wasn't being stared down by a rotting corpse. She stood up and peered through the window.

"I can't see anything from here. It's too dark."

"Okay. That's okay. Let's do this another way. Where in the house are you?"

Agent Clark Weston was motioning for another agent to come to his desk. Agent Shane Billford stopped talking to his acquaintance and headed over to see what he wanted. Weston placed his hand over the phone and whispered to Billford, "I think we either have a genuine nutcase or this is a real emergency."

Ellen answered. "I'm in the kitchen."

"That's good. Now, when you look directly to your right, what is the first thing you see?"

"A china cabinet, a table, and four chairs that match each other. And a dead woman sitting in one of the chairs."

"And what do you see to your left?"

"A sink, a dish drain, a set of windows."

"Okay. What we need to do—"

"Oh, God! No! No!"

Ellen was listening to instructions from Weston when headlights beamed across the kitchen wall and alerted her that Freddy was home.

"What's happening, ma'am?"

"He's home! He just came back home! What do I do? Help me, please! Please help me!"

Agent Weston could hear the panic in Ellen's voice and knew she was being truthful.

"You need to get out of the house. Find a safe exit and run."

Ellen didn't have time to listen. She didn't have time to do anything at this point. She decided to run back to where Cathy was. For some reason, even if it did sound morbid, she felt safer near her friend.

Freddy entered through the kitchen and slammed the door shut behind him. The sound echoed through the whole first level. The sound made Ellen jump. She looked around and decided to do what she hoped would save her in the end.

She sat beside Cathy, looking up at the ceiling and sitting perfectly still. Maybe Freddy's mind was warped to the point that she could *pretend* to be dead. Maybe he would think he'd slipped off into a daze again and he would try to remember that he'd already killed her. Ellen knew nothing about dead people, rigor mortis, or anything of the sort. So she did what her instinct told her to do.

When Freddy walked in, she heard him slide a chair from the kitchen table. He began to talk to the unfortunate woman beside him.

"She's gone, Paula. She's gone. I let her get away from me. Lori will be so disappointed in me."

"Lori loves you, Freddy. She'll understand. You know that. Just find a replacement, that's all." Freddy used a lower voice for Paula. It wasn't much higher pitched than his own voice.

"Are you sure?"

"Of course I'm sure. Go talk to her. Tell her the truth. The love you two share could never die, right?"

Freddy smiled at Paula. "You are so smart. I'm so glad you can talk to me and calm me down. Well, wish me luck."

As Freddy pushed up on the table, he said "good luck, baby" in Paula's voice. He walked into the living room to where Lori, Cathy, and Ellen sat. His head started to spin. His face contorted into a look of pain as he stared directly down at Ellen. He couldn't remember embalming her, much less bringing her inside.

He had broken his pattern. He and Lori always, always made love with new friends right away, while they were still in the building. He could not recall bringing Lori out or Ellen in.

Freddy grabbed the door frame and held on for support. His world was slinging him around in circles and he felt woozy.

After what felt like two or three full minutes to Ellen, Freddy sat down beside her. He was between Lori and Ellen, while Cathy still spilled out across the floor.

"Lori? You've met Ellen?"

"Yes, dear. I did. Don't you remember bringing her in?"

"Of course I do. What do you think of her?"

"She's as beautiful as you said she was, Freddy. I love her! And I love you!"

Ellen was horrified by what she heard. Freddy's voice went from low to high, from high to low. His voice changed to accommodate Lori. She wanted to look at him, but dared not move even her eyes. When she could tell he was moving or twitching a little, she blinked. She was doing whatever it took to survive. If that meant a sitting statue-like with a non-blinking stare, then that's what she'd do. Her eyes were stinging and she could feel the tears welling up again. She tried to think of anything that would prevent them from rolling down her cheeks.

When Freddy leaned in to kiss Lori, it was so hard not to heave. But she managed to control that, too.

It wasn't until she heard zippers and snaps and buttons flying loose that she really had a hard time. He stood and pulled down his pants, then lowered Lori's pants down around her ankles. He picked her up and allowed the jeans to slowly hit the floor. As Freddy lay down, he held Lori up over him. He slowly lowered her down and Ellen knew exactly what was happening, even if she'd never done this.

The moans and breathing alternated between high and low sounds for what Ellen estimated to be twenty or thirty minutes. Then, Freddy got on knees and rolled Cathy over. She was now staring right at Ellen. The tears came uncontrollably as she watched Freddy mount her best friend.

The worst was yet to come for Ellen. Freddy laid on the floor, a girl on each side and he began to talk to Ellen.

"See what you've been missing, babe? We're just all one happy family here and we share our love. It's the most beautiful thing in the world."

"Yes, it is, Ellen," Freddy imitated Cathy's voice. The similarity was uncanny. Ellen felt as if Cathy was the one talking.

"Come join us, Ellen." Lori spoke through Freddy.

"Is that what you ladies want? She's still very new. Not even stiff yet. Her body temperature is still warm. Are you sure?"

Ellen heard one of the three or Freddy, or whoever give a moan of approval.

"Well, if that's what Lori wants, that's what Lori gets."

Ellen lay mortified as Freddy lifted her from the sofa. He stroked her head and face and began kissing her neck.

He groped her small breasts through the blouse she wore. He unbuttoned her jeans and pulled them down, revealing smooth and creamy legs. He pulled her legs apart and gently lay down on her. As he was about to guide himself in, Ellen closed her eyes.

How can I possibly lay helplessly still and have my body violated like this?

Just before Freddy entered her, she snapped out of the horror induced trance she was in. *I won't!*

Ellen brought her knee up and thrust it hard into Freddy's groin. The sound he made was that of confusion and pain. She rolled over, stood, and found her best stance to fight the lunatic off.

"Come on, you son of a bitch!" she yelled at him.

Freddy was still lying helpless on the floor, writhing in pain from the unexpected blow.

"Get up! Get up, you sick twisted sorry excuse for a man! Get up and fight!"

Freddy held the floor tightly and pushed himself up. "You're dead!" he shouted out in angry confusion.

Ellen laughed. "No, you are!" and she kicked him high up on his chest.

Freddy couldn't breathe. He couldn't move.

Ellen kicked him again and again until he was sprawled out on the floor, wincing. He brought his legs up and hugged his knees tightly. But Ellen felt no pity on him. She pounced on him with all her weight and hit, kicked, and scratched at him. When he quit defending himself, she pulled on her pants and ran. She never slowed down running, even though her whole body was shivering in fear and exhaustion.

She found the road and ran until her heart felt that it would burst in her chest. She felt victory at the sight of car lights heading directly toward her. She threw her arms up and began to swing them back and forth.

"Stop! Help me!" she screamed. The night air was cold and she saw her own breath escape in a fog around her mouth.

The car skidded to a stop, and a man rolled down his window. "What the hell happened to you, little missy?"

Ellen wasn't thinking as she ran around to the passenger side door. This could also be a deranged psychopath, but he couldn't be any worse than what she had behind her.

"I need help! The man that lives up there, Freddy? He's crazy! He tried to kill me! Please! Help me!" She could smell beer when she opened the door. The smell kind of oozed out around her, but she flopped down, anyway.

"Okay, okay. Calm down a little."

Ellen could have punched him, too. She couldn't calm down. *Why did people always say that during a crisis?*

As the car rolled on down the road, Ellen frantically searched for an open restaurant, a bar, anywhere she could call for help. "Where are we? What town are we in?" Ellen didn't mean to yell, but she did.

"Wadesboro," the man answered.

"What state?"

"North Carolina."

"Oh, North Carolina. I'm from Oakdale. I don't know how far away that is from here. I'm lost. Freddy took me."

"Freddy? You talkin' 'bout Fredlee?"

"Who?"

"Fredlee. He runs the funeral home. He don't bother nobody. He ain't dangerous or nothin'. Just a little different, that's all."

Ellen saw lights up ahead and realized they were entering city limits. Cars sped by and trucks rolled past. She was finally safe.

Chapter Thirty-Two

Betsy sat quietly as Harold drove along Highway 74. The road seemed darker than ever. They were one hundred miles from home when the headlights shown on a car parked on the shoulder. Betsy gasped as they neared the car. It was so similar to Ellen's.

"Stay in the car, Bet," Harold murmured.

Betsy sat still and looking on at that empty car.

Oh, please God, don't let that be Ellen's car and if it is, please don't let her be hurt.

Harold was looking in through the driver's door. He couldn't see anything that looked suspicious or out of place. He made his way around to the passenger's side and that's when he noticed the flat. He made his way back to his own car, grabbed a flashlight and headed back again. Betsy was asking him if it was Ellen's car, but he ignored her.

Betsy jumped out and ran to her husband's side. He was knelt down, shining the light on the tire. He immediately noticed the small hole, but kept that information to himself. Someone had tampered with his daughter's tire. He popped the trunk to find it barren. No bags, no suitcases, no spare.

Harold shut the lid down and looked to Betsy. "We're going to the police station."

When they were back inside their car, Harold took a map from the glove compartment. He turned it this way and that until he'd found the area he was searching for. He studied the lines and curves and finally cranked up.

"Two miles south of here. She was only two miles from the local police station."

"Harold? What do you think happened?"

Harold considered sharing his thoughts, but decided against that. Betsy didn't need to know what he was really thinking.

"I think her tire went flat and someone offered her a ride, Betsy. I think she's safe and sound somewhere out here. We've just got to have a little help finding her, that's all."

Betsy shuddered. She'd been married for twenty-three years and she knew when her husband was lying.

Not that he'd lied to her often. In fact, the last time she caught him in a bind it was over how much money he'd spent on her Christmas gift. But he was lying to her now to keep her calm.

"That's not what you're thinking, Harold. But that's okay. I'm thinking the worst, too. Maybe it's best if we don't say those things out loud. It would be too final if we did."

That was when Betsy broke down. Her cries were loud and full of fear and worry. She had known since nine o'clock that something was wrong. And now her fears were confirmed.

"We don't know what happened, Betsy. Let's just stay positive and calm. I'm sure Ellie is fine."

Betsy only nodded her head. She fumbled around in her purse, pulled out a pack of Marlboros, and lit one up.

"Don't start now, Harold. You can complain later, but not now." She spoke through a mouthful of smoke. She'd hid this nasty habit for over a year, but now she just didn't care if he did know.

"I'm not saying a thing. In fact, light one for me, too."

Betsy grinned a small, crooked grin and handed it to Harold. Then she lit another and blew out a much needed breath of filtered nicotine.

Harold turned left at the first light they reached. According to the map, the police department would be two blocks down. He pulled the car around, searching for a parking space. The lot was practically empty, so it wasn't a hard task.

Betsy glanced at her watch. Five A.M. The sun would be rising soon. It had been a long night and Saturday morning didn't promise to be better.

As they trudged across the vacant lot, they both threw down what was left of their cigarettes and Harold held open the glass door. Betsy walked in first. Spotting a pay phone, she reached for a dime and headed over to call the boys.

"Hello?" Daniel answered before the first ring could completely sound.

"Daniel Kelly. You should be asleep."

"Where's Ellen? Is everything okay?"

"Daniel, can you put Mary or Jackson on for a sec?"

"Mom? Is Ellen okay?"

"Daniel, I'm sure she's fine. We found her car, so that's good. She had a flat."

"But you didn't find her?"

Betsy closed her eyes and held back the tears once again.

"We're working on it, kiddo. Now, put Mary on, please?"

Daniel was also crying when he handed the phone to Mary.

"Hello? Betsy? How are things?"

"Hi, Mary. We don't know much yet. Her car was parked on the side of the road. She had a flat. Harold and I are thinking she probably took a ride from someone to get help. She's probably on her way back with a spare now."

"Oh, well, that's good, right?"

"Yes, I think so. How are the boys?"

"Worried, but fine. We've actually had a lot of fun together."

"I can't thank you enough for this. Really, Mary, thank you."

Mary wished her luck, made Betsy promise to call back soon, and placed the orange receiver back on its cradle. Betsy stood still for another moment before turning to Harold. They had both hoped that Ellen would be home by now, picked up by someone trusting. But Mary had heard nothing from Ellen or the Oakdale Police Department.

Ahead of them were three doors. The windows on each were painted with block style lettering. The first door was identified as "**homicide**." The second was "**booking**" and the third was "**Inquisitions.**"

They stood staring at those doors and finally, Harold opened the door labeled inquisitions. Neither of them were sure what that even meant, but it was better than homicide and they weren't being booked.

Two black sofas lined the hallway. Stiff, imitation leather with ashtrays on either side. The whole building was bland and official looking. They walked up to a counter where a woman in a blue uniform stood writing something on a pink sheet of paper. Another officer sat at a desk to their right. To their left was a brown paneled wall with a row of black and white pictures hanging together. Each one was a policeman, holding a hat in hand.

Underneath those were pictures of newspaper clippings. Some were highlighted with headlines reading things like *'Officer Saves Boy Trapped In Flooded Car'*, *'Daring Policeman Risks Life to Rescue Elderly Woman from Burning Building'*, and *'Cops Save the Day!'*. Some were yellowed by years behind frames, but both Harold and Betsy got the feeling not too much tragedy had hit this college town in the past.

"How can I help you?" the officer behind the counter asked.

Harold started by explaining that Ellen had never come home. He continued on about the car, the flat and the fact that he himself had checked her spare before she left the weekend before. The officer listened intently.

"She's been missing since what? Around nine last night?"

Harold nodded. "'Bout nine, maybe ten. She's usually home no later than that."

"And she's nineteen?"

"Yes, ma'am."

"Then technically, she's not missing. You can file a missing persons report at, we'll say nine tonight."

Betsy grunted loudly enough for everyone to hear her. The female officer looked at her, not at all impressed.

"Look, I'm sorry. I know how you feel—"

Betsy cut her off. "Do you? Do you know how I feel? My daughter has never just up and left. She would never just leave her car on the roadside. She would call, if she could. You have no idea how I feel!" Betsy shouted.

"Raising your voice at me will not help you, ma'am. You'll only spend the day here with us, locked in a holding cell. Is that what you want?"

"Unbelievable. Just unbelievable," Harold muttered.

He pulled on Betsy's elbow and the two walked away. When they were back out in the foyer, he walked over to the plain, black sofa. The wooden frame cracked when he sat down in it.

"Harold, what on earth are we going to do?"

He only shook his head. He had never felt so helpless before in all his life. He pulled a Camel from inside his jacket pocket and fired it up. Betsy looked at him quizzically.

"Don't start on me, Betsy. You can fuss all you like when this is over, but not now."

The two of them gave a half nervous laugh and Betsy sat down beside him. She placed her hand on his knee and lay her head over on his shoulder.

Just as she sighed a deep breath, two officers came running through the foyer from a side door that was unlabeled. There was no window on it, either. The sound made Betsy raise her head. They were having an emergency somewhere, but just not here. If only they would run like that to find her daughter.

Soon after, another two cops came out. Then it was like fire ants boiling from a hill. They counted seven in all. It seemed like so many more, with their loud voices and heavy boots on the hard flooring. Betsy and Harold looked at them as they ran out of the building. When the glass doors shut behind the last one, it was silent all over again. It remained still and silent in that hallway as Betsy and Harold brainstormed. They were at a loss and in a strange town with only strangers to depend on.

Suddenly, the door marked *Inquisitions* opened and an officer stepped out into the hallway.

"I figured you had left by now."

"And go where?" Harold asked.

The officer considered that question before answering. "I apologize for being so useless. It's just that we do have a protocol to follow. Can you both come with me, please?"

Harold and Betsy followed the officer into a private room to the rear of the counter where the female officer stood. She was still doing paperwork.

"Please, have a seat." The officer motioned at two chairs on the other side of his desk.

"Can you describe your daughter? What she was wearing when she left this evening? Hair color? Maybe any visible birthmarks?"

"Oh, God. You've found her. Is she dead?"

"We have a young woman four counties over claiming to be a Miss Ellen Kelly." He fumbled through paperwork until he'd found the information. Harold and Betsy both began to cry.

"That's our daughter's name! Is she okay?"

"She is being sent to the Anson County Hospital for evaluation. That's all I really know."

"How do we get there?" Betsy shouted out in relief.

"Officer Timmons is going to lead you there. She is getting some paperwork together now to take with you. I'll just need you to sign some papers. All it says is that you were here, problem was resolved, and you are releasing us of any liability."

"Oh, sure. Whatever we need to do," Harold said through tears and a very trembling voice.

The policeman shook his hand, nodded to Betsy, and showed them back out to where Officer Timmons was waiting. She didn't speak until they were out in the foyer once again.

"I'll drive with my lights on, but no siren. I won't go too fast so that you can follow in behind me. It's about a two hour drive from here."

"Yeah, fine. Thank you," was all either of them could say. Whatever exhaustion they felt earlier was now relieved through adrenaline.

"The boys! I need to call the boys!" Betsy exclaimed.

Officer Timmons stopped at the pay phone hanging on the wall. She handed Betsy a dime and smiled. "Go ahead. It's okay. Do what you need to do."

Betsy took the dime from the officer and quickly dialed home. Mary answered. "Hello?"

"Hi, Mary! They found her! The police found Ellen. We are on our way to get her now. She's in, what county?" She looked at Timmons.

"Anson," Timmons whispered.

"She's in Anson County and they have her in the hospital. I don't know what happened yet, but we are on our way now! Daniel and Gaige okay?"

"Daniel fell asleep watching T.V. about an hour ago and Gaige is asleep beside him on the floor. Should I wake them?"

"Oh, no. Let them sleep. But when they wake, tell them we'll be home soon with Ellen," Betsy said with a relieved smiled that Mary could hear over the phone line.

The call was disconnected and Betsy turned to face Harold, who was also smiling. A minute later, they were in the car and following Officer Timmons out on to Hwy. 74, headed east toward Anson County.

Chapter Thirty-Three

Freddy slowly stood. He assessed the situation with an irate emotion. The room was spinning. Ellen was gone. How had this happened?

He shook Lori so fiercely that her blonde wig fell to the floor. His mind raced in a million directions.

"Why did this happen, Lori? What has happened?"

Lori didn't respond.

Hey, Fredlee! I know what happened.

Freddy spun around and looked to see his reflection in a mirror hanging on the living room wall. His reflection had its back to him.

You worthless hunk of shit! This is all your fault! Our plan is ruined and it's all your fault!

Freddy had not heard his inside-voice in so long, it startled him. Slowly, his image turned to face him. He was taken aback by what he saw. There was no face. Just a blank, hazy spot where Freddy's face should be.

"I didn't mean to. I swear. It was an accident."

Well, hot shit. What are you going to do? How 'ya gonna fix this mess? I tell you what. You've got to leave. Leave it all behind. Just go!

Freddy's neck began to twist and turn as his inside-voice insulted him again and again.

"I can't leave Lori!"

You never had Lori! You had an imitation makeshift bitch. That was all you could ever have, you dog.

Freddy considered the words in his mind. He was right, too. This wasn't Lori. It never had been.

Why hadn't he seen that before? Freddy began to knock over lamps and tables. He threw a porcelain vase into the mirror and watched as the pieces fell around his bare feet. Shards of glass punctured his toes and the tops of his feet, but he felt nothing, absolutely nothing.

He tossed anything he could find and watched things crash all around him. When there was nothing else to break, he stumbled in to the kitchen and did it over again. From one room to another, he destroyed his surroundings as Ellen had destroyed him.

He clumsily climbed the stairs, knocking pictures off the walls as he went. He was crying loudly and moaning a sound so mournful that anyone hearing it would have no doubt of his pain. Only there was no one around to sympathize with Freddy Lee. There was no one there to feel his agony, not even his precious, beloved Lori.

He slid down the wall in his bedroom. Across from him sat Rebecca Lewis. He never even asked her name. He only knew it now because of the newspaper clippings. She'd been hidden in the attic, but eventually Freddy could stand it no longer. He had dragged her down and placed her in his room.

"What the hell are you looking at?"

The corpse never spoke.

"I said, what are you looking at? You nameless whore!"

Freddy kicked the chair and watched the woman fall to the floor. When her limb body slumped down, he kicked her over and over again.

Freddy knocked his fist into the wall, hitting it again and again. When his fists were raw, he pulled himself up and repeatedly kicked the wall with bloody, bare feet.

His moans sounded like metal grinding against metal, or a building collapsing. His world was indeed collapsing around him. When his tired legs could kick no more, he fell across his bed and wailed out into the empty house.

He knew Ellen would get help. He knew she was bringing pigs out here. He could just see the look on people's faces as they crowded around to see what he had been busy doing over the years.

* * * * * * * *

Anson Community Hospital
Wadesboro, NC
February 18, 1978

Ellen was screaming so loudly she could be heard down the hallway leading in to the emergency room. Her cries echoed on the mint green walls that flowed into the corridor.

Doctor Wiles hurried in to where Ellen was laying. Her arms and legs were restrained and her bald head moved back and forth uncontrollably.

"Untie her! Let her up!" Dr. Wiles yelled to the nurse in attendance.

"But Dr. Wiles, she's hysterical! If we let her up, she'll cause harm to herself, possibly us!"

Dr. Wiles was a matter-of-fact kind of man. He didn't wait for the nurse. He began to untie Ellen himself. "Get out!" he yelled to the nurse.

She'd never been yelled at before, but then again, she'd never argued with a doctor before, either. She held her head down and quietly excused herself.

Ellen calmed down as soon as her arms and legs were loosened.

"Thank you," was all she could manage to strangle out.

"I'm Dr. Wiles. I need to know what has happened. Where do you hurt, miss?"

"Nowhere. I'm fine. He didn't hurt me. He shaved my head and was going to hurt me, rape me even, but I got away."

Dr. Wiles carefully examined Ellen. He shone a bright light in her eyes, felt for her reflexes, and spoke softly to her. When he had done everything that he needed to do, he pulled a rolling stool next to her. He listened intently as she described the horrors she'd seen.

Three nurses stood outside the closed off section in the E.R. Only a thick, white curtain separated Ellen from a drunk with a skinned forehead and a broken arm.

Across the room, another section was closed off. On the other side of that curtain, lay a mother having semi-severe labor pains. Her husband was counting to ten with her every time she felt a contraction coming on. The noises were loud, so the nurses had to strain to hear Ellen.

One nurse gasped as Ellen described the women in Freddy's home.

"Fredlee? Is she talking about Fredlee?"

Another nurse shook her head. "It couldn't be Fredlee. He couldn't harm a flea."

The third nurse just stood with her hands over her mouth.

When Dr. Wiles stepped around the divider, he saw the nurses gathered and ordered a tranquilizer to be given to Ellen. Ellen had already been in observation for three hours and Dr. Wiles was headed to the phone to contact the police department when the glass doors shoved open.

Betsy and Harold Kelly ran down the green corridor, past a vending machine and coffee maker. They only slowed down when they had gone as far as they could. A nurse held out her arms and stopped them.

"Whoa! How can I help you?" she asked.

"Ellen Kelly. We are the parents of Ellen Kelly. Where is our daughter?"

Dr. Wiles intercepted the three people and took Harold by the arm. "Mr. Kelly, I'm Dr. Wiles, the E.R. on-call doctor this evening. I have Ellen in a closed off section for emergency observation."

"How is she? Is she hurt?" Betsy begged of the doctor.

"She is stable, but a sedative has been given. She doesn't appear to have any injuries, other than a scrape on her head, some bruises and, well—"

"Well what?" Harold interrupted.

"The man who took Ellen shaved her head. She is completely bald."

"Bald? Why? Who would shave her head?" Betsy wondered aloud.

"The police department has been notified and they have dispatch officers to the scene. We'll get the person responsible for this, but the main thing now is to be very patient with Ellen. She was in a terrible situation and needs her rest. She was restrained while she was being kept, so try not to make her feel trapped by crowding her. I've ordered a batch of blood work, just in case and while she's out of it, I'd like to do a full body scan, check for any broken bones I may have missed during the initial examination."

"Whatever you need to do, doc," Harold agreed.

"When can we see her?" Betsy pleaded.

"You can go right on in," Dr. Wiles responded.

He led the way to the section where Ellen was now sleeping peacefully.

At first, there was shock at seeing her with no hair, but they were thankful to have their daughter back safe. Betsy sat on the edge of the bed and looked down at Ellen's arms. She was covered in bruises and had burn marks where she'd pulled so hard to free herself of Freddy's leather straps.

Betsy sat quietly and cried as her daughter slept. Harold stood beside her and he too cried tears of joy.

One Grave Secret

Chapter Thirty-Four

Detective Leland was quiet for most of the trip back to Anson County. Celeste was equally exhausted and frustrated. Their trip to Maxton had turned out to be in vain. There were no more clues there than there had been all along.

"Sooner or later—" Celeste began again. Leland interrupted her.

"Yeah, I know. Sooner or later."

Leland was in a foul mood. Celeste quieted and looked out the window.

When Leland's radio blared, they both jumped.

"10-10," the operator said.

Leland turned up the volume to listen in as the code used meant *possible crime in progress.*

"That's a 10-6, all units stand by."

Leland looked at Celeste, who didn't seem to give the announcement much consideration. It could mean anything from a home invasion to a store robbery. They were out of Leland's jurisdiction either way.

When the operator's voice crackled over the airwaves again, Leland pulled over to listen intently.

"10-71, over."

"I don't recognize that one. What's it mean?" Celeste asked.

"It means there is a citywide emergency."

Leland picked up the radio and pressed the *transmit* button. "Detective Leland requesting address. Over." Static filled the radio before a voice came through loud and clear.

"All officers respond to 228, Elm Grove Road, over."

Leland turned the cruiser around and turned on the siren. The car sped quickly towards Lee and Son Funeral Home and Chapel.

"Elm Grove? Wonder what in the world?"

Celeste held on tightly as Leland took curves at top speed. Then he pictured the street in his mind.

"The funeral home? Isn't that 228? I sure hope Fredlee is okay."

Celeste thought for a moment and remembered that Fredlee had taken over his dad's funeral home just after Mr. Fred had died. He had taken care of everything for her when her mother passed away. The Lee family was a wonderful asset to the community.

"I sure hope no one has hurt poor Fredlee," she said while grasping the seat around her.

"But a 10-71? I don't think I've heard that one over the radio before," Leland added.

Another minute had passed when an officer spoke into the radio, confirming the dispatcher's communication. Mark Leland suddenly had butterflies when he saw the plume of smoke rising from the Lee home.

Chapter Thirty-Five

"Back up requested at 228, Elm Grove Road, over," the officer said into his radio. Other cops were already on the scene, but more help was needed.

"Officer reporting a 10-70," said another cop at the scene.

Freddy's house was ablaze and there was nothing the policemen could do but wait for firefighters to respond.

"That's a 10-39, over." The dispatcher confirmed that the message had been delivered to the local fire department.

The sirens wailed through the early morning of Saturday, February 18. People were piling out of houses up and down the road and making their way to the Lee home. The blazes were too hot for officers to try and get inside.

Freddy wouldn't allow them to take his Lori, despite what his inside-voice said. He wouldn't go down like the fuzz would want. He was in control and he would control his own destiny.

When the fire trucks arrived, they hurriedly began to douse the flames. There would be nothing left of Lee and Son Funeral Parlor and Chapel. All that could be done was to control the fire from spreading to neighboring homes.

By ten o'clock, all that remained of the fire was a smoky, sooty mess. Firefighters rummaged through the ashes, finding the charred remains of seven bodies.

It would be days, possibly weeks before the remains could be identified. And that would depend on dental records, if available. Even though Ellen had seen Cathy's remains in the house already, nothing official could be confirmed without the coroner's release.

* * * * * * * *

In the moments before Freddy ignited the flame, he gathered his girls together in what was left of the den. He could hear glass and splinters of wood crunching beneath his feet. He thought it odd that he felt no discomfort. He was numb now, through and through.

He carefully replaced Lori's wig.

"Perfect. Now, I've got beautiful attire for each of you." The house remained quiet. Not even Lori responded.

Freddy hastily dressed all of his girls in long, flowing evening gowns, something he had saved for the perfect occasion. The box he took them from wasn't empty, though. One gown remained. The baby blue gown he'd reserved for Ellen lay in the bottom.

When the girls had been dressed in what he considered their very best, he tossed the box aside.

"No use in crying over spilled milk, right?"

He sat down at Lori's feet and gently laid his head in her lap. The cries he made now were quiet, low hums.

"Lori, you must be brave now. Our time together is over, you know that. All good things must come to an end, or so they say." He looked up, expecting Lori to respond and when she didn't, he felt the rage spilling out again.

"Fine. Have it your way. I tried. God knows, I tried. I just wanted to say goodbye. I wanted to tell you how sorry I am. I wanted to tell you I love you, Lori."

Lori and the others just sat, staring off at things that Freddy could not see. He took the matches and struck one.

He held the flame at the bottom of Lori's gown and watched as it was quickly engulfed with a hot glow of yellow. Then he turned to Paula and did the same thing. He sat back on his heels as her purple gown fired into something hot and mesmerizing.

When he reached Michelle, he touched her head, rubbed the smooth lump of skin on the side of her face where her ear had once been.

"I'm sorry, Michelle."

When he got no response, he held a match under the skirt of a gorgeous pink frill of fabric. Amber, Cathy, Lisa, and Rebecca all lit the room in a fantastic color of fire. Freddy stood there, unresponsive until a small flame licked his arm. That brought him back to the present and he rushed upstairs.

He knew he only had seconds, so he hurried as fast as he could. He threw some things into a suitcase and rushed back downstairs.

Freddy made his way into the room where his girls were ablaze. He only stood still for a moment before leaving.

The only thing he felt now was anger at the girls who, until now, thought he could do no wrong. They had each told him how perfect he was. And now they just sat, burning brightly and watching his dreams melt away.

Freddy grabbed the suitcase and a bank bag of cash and gingerly walked away from the disaster. He was singing *Stayin' Alive* again as he headed to the bus stop. He knew the cops would be here soon enough, but it would take time to get Ellen calm enough to talk, and the fuzz would need time to realize the town freak really was capable after all. He smiled to himself as he did his best strut.

He was at the bus stop in less than ten minutes. He heard the Greyhound screeching to a halt just moments after he arrived. *Impeccable timing, I swear!*

Freddy never looked back on Wadesboro as the bus pulled away from the curve. He only saw two things. His reflection in the window had returned and he smiled at himself with confidence. And he saw blue lights heading toward his house.

Lee and Son Funeral Parlor and Chapel are no more, he thought as his head grew heavy on his shoulders and his thoughts grew heavy in his mind. He closed his eyes and allowed the humming of the bus to lull him to sleep.

Chapter Thirty-Six

Ellen opened very tired eyes to find her mother sitting in a recliner near her bed. "Mom?"

Betsy popped up immediately and was at her daughter's side. "Good morning, sweetheart!"

"How, well, when did you get here?"

Betsy smiled as she took a place on the edge of the bed. "Last night. Right after you were brought in. Your dad and I had looked for you everywhere."

Betsy rubbed her hand down Ellen's arm, and then stopped where an I.V. was fed into her hand. Ellen was very groggy.

Some memories from last night were too hazy, as if it was all just a dream. She placed a hand on her head and when she felt the slickness instead of locks of hair, she remembered that it wasn't a dream at all.

"My hair—" she started to say.

Betsy placed a finger over her daughter's lips. "Shh, it will grow back. You know that."

Ellen smiled. She had thought the same thing as Freddy was shaving her. "It's just hair, right?"

Betsy smiled and nodded. She held back the tears now. Ellen had been through a terrible ordeal and she would try her best to be strong for her only daughter.

"Where's daddy?"

"He drove home this morning to pick up Daniel and Gaige and get you some clean fresh clothes. They're all coming back together so we can take you home."

Ellen lay back on her pillow. She had so many questions, but couldn't think of where to start. Then she remembered something very important. "Peter!"

Betsy slightly laughed. "Don't worry, he knows you're fine and he's coming, too. Your dad gave very good directions and we're sure he'll be here by this afternoon."

"Yeah, I bet. Dad probably gave him directions to get him a hundred miles farther away!"

The two women were laughing when a nurse entered the room.

Ellen had been placed in a private room just after all her test came back good. No broken bones, no concussion, nothing to worry about.

Whitney smiled at her patient. Whitney Robsteck was a very good nurse and took pride in her position. She cared for each patient with dignity and respect. She actually felt honored to be the nurse on call this morning. Ellen Kelly was quite the local celebrity.

"Sounds like someone is feeling much better!" Whitney exclaimed cheerfully

"I'm sore and I feel like I've been hit by a Mack truck, but yeah, I'm much better."

Whitney smiled down at Ellen. "Well, from what I hear, you beat the crap of that freak, Fredlee."

"You mean Freddy?"

Whitney realized that only locals had ever called him Fredlee, and she nodded. "You really should consider a career in boxing!"

Whitney checked Ellen's vitals, applied ointment to the gash on her forehead and the burn on her leg. After she had replaced her I.V. bag, she smiled at Ellen and turned to go.

"When can I go home?"

Whitney turned and looked back at Ellen. "Well, it's not for me to say. But by the looks of things, you should be out of here very soon. The doctor will be in soon to check on you and he'll be able to tell you for sure. For now, just rest and try to relax."

The nurse looked to Betsy. "If either of you need anything at all, just let me know, okay?"

Betsy shook her head and thanked Whitney for being so kind.

"Oh, it's my pleasure. Take care, Ellen." Whitney was still smiling when she left the room.

* * * * * * * *

Detective Mark Leland was packing up the last of the notes he had on the Lee file when Celeste knocked on his office door. He looked up and smiled at his secretary.

"By now you should know you don't have to knock, Celeste."

"Just on my way out for the night. Thought I'd stop by and see if you need anything else. You good?"

"Never better. I just can't get Fredlee out of my mind. I never would've thought it of him. Not in a million years would I have thought him capable of something like this."

Celeste took a breath. "I know. I was just up there last fall when mom passed. He was the nicest thing. So professional and sincere."

"Guess it goes to show that you just never really know a person, huh?"

Celeste took a seat near Leland. "You had no way of knowing, Mark."

"I talked to him, Celeste. The night of the candle light vigil for Trish Colbert. I talked to the sick monster myself."

"Lots of people did. You can't blame yourself." If it makes you feel any better, the Colbert family will be here in the morning. You can finally give them the closer that they need."

The detective had arrived on the scene as the fire department was dousing the last of the flames inside the Lee home. He had stayed on location as the remains of seven bodies were removed. There were seven bodies that he had searched for. Unless someone else had taken one of those women, there was the possibility that Fredlee wasn't even in there.

"I won't feel like it's completely over until I hear from the coroner," Leland said, his voice sounding weary.

Celeste nodded in agreement. They couldn't even call the Colbert family until the remains were all identified. She wanted nothing more than to give each family the closure they deserved.

Only time would tell. It would prove to be a very long, exhausting wait.

* * * * * * * *

Ellen smiled. She didn't know what she wanted to do in the distant future, but right now all she wanted to do was be with her family and Peter. Those were the people who mattered now. Even Daniel and Gaige were special to her.

Daniel and Gaige grew closer than they ever expected they would. They actually had a respect for their sister they had never had before. They were really a little scared of her after she told them how she took down a mad man.

It took months of therapy for Ellen to really come to terms with what had happened to her. It was hard accepting Cathy's death, too. Ellen Kelly was a strong woman and she didn't fear what was out in the world, just what was frozen in her mind and entered her dreams almost nightly.

There was one dream that reoccurred over and over. She could see Freddy coming at her with a scalpel. A big grin covered his face. He moved closer and closer to Ellen and when he was finally inches from her face, it was actually Cathy. Ellen woke up wet with sweat every time that dream came.

At first, she would wake the whole house up with her screams, but now she just woke herself up, wringing wet with perspiration, her heart pounding and her body quivering. She would lay there in the dark, reciting what her therapist had recommended.

"I am Ellen Elizabeth Kelly. I am alive. Freddy Lee is dead. I am safe and I am alive."

She had also added Psalm 23 to her mantra. Ellen had found that her faith was bigger than her fears.

Chapter Thirty-Seven

State Coroner's office
Raleigh, NC

Doctor Randy Godwin examined the remains of seven bodies transferred there overnight. It was a messy job any time there were burned victims involved.

"Case number 90254, body burned beyond obvious recognition. Estimated age seventeen to twenty-one. Bones intact. Pelvis indicates victim was a female who had never given birth. Traces of detrepanol in deep tissue. Right ear nonexistent. Dental records confirm body to be that of Erin Underhill."

"Case number 90255, body burned beyond obvious recognition. Estimated age, seventeen to twenty-one. Bones recovered, not intact. Pelvis indicates victim was a female who had never given birth. Traces of detrepanol in bone samples. Right ear nonexistent. Dental records confirm body to be that of Michelle Carthage."

The coroner continued through three days of labor to identify the bodies of Rebecca Lewis, Lisa, Amber, Paula, and Cathy. Each were the same, with the exception of Paula Herst.

Dr. Godwin could tell that she was the only woman to have delivered a baby. All seven women had large traces of detrepanol in what was left of their deep tissue or bone marrow. The right ear of each corpse had been removed.

When Dr. Godwin called Leland, the detective slammed the phone down. Celeste came running in to see what the fuss was about.

"He's gone, Celeste. There were seven bodies, all women. Autopsies confirm the detrepanol. That's what Ellen described. She remembered a needle in the car and the feeling of complete numbness for a while after that. That's how he got 'em, Celeste. He had to drug them."

From what Ellen had told him during interviews, Freddy had shot her full of something that knocked her out cold. When she came to, she was strapped down and completely vulnerable.

Autopsies also found that the women had been embalmed. There was no way for him to know if that was done before or after death, but Ellen had described the medical equipment. They would keep that information from the victim's families. They had been through enough.

That was all Leland needed to know to confirm that Freddy had also taken Trish Colbert. If it had not been for Ellen's memory, they would have never known why he dumped her. Ellen had provided several pieces to an otherwise distorted puzzle.

After digging through piles of records, a connection was made between Lori Eades and the victims. Leland knew from Ellen that Freddy had fallen in love with Lori's corpse and had replaced her with all of these women.

After Roger Eades signed the consent form, Lori Eades' body was exhumed. The Eades family could at least rest knowing that she had not previously been disturbed. There was speculation about Freddy committing necrophilia with her body, but Roger didn't want further testing to be performed. His daughter had suffered enough.

Detective Mark Leland would never rest until he tracked down this disturbed man. He knew Fredlee was out there somewhere and would make it his life's mission to find him and make him suffer the way so many others had suffered at his hands.

Friday, April 14, 1978

Peter and Ellen walked hand in hand across campus. This was her first weekend back and away from her family. Harold and Betsy had both fallen in love with Peter and he'd promised to take very good care of Ellen.

When they were in front of the accounting department, Peter reminded Ellen of the time she tossed her cookies right on the steps there.

"Ugh! Don't remind me!"

"You should love that memory," Peter whispered down at her. "This is where we first met." He gave her a soft, slow kiss.

He looked around for a moment, as if he was nervous about something.

"What's wrong, Peter?"

"Nothing at all." As he spoke he began to fold down, finding balance on one knee. He fumbled in his pocket and took Ellen's hand when he'd found what he was hunting.

"Ellen, I love you."

Ellen could feel her face turning from its usual fair tone to a deep red.

"I love you, too, Peter."

He opened his hand, revealing a beautiful diamond ring. On either side was a smaller diamond. The light caught it at just the right moment and Ellen gasped.

"Ellen, you could make me the happiest man on earth, if you would be my wife. Will you marry me?"

"Oh, my, Peter! Yes! Yes! I will marry you!"

As she answered, people began to applaud. She looked around in surprise. She had been lost in Peter and never noticed the crowd forming around them.

Peter stood and held her tightly in his arms as the crowd began to disperse. When Ellen pulled away and looked at him, he had a tear rolling down his face. She gently rubbed it away and kissed him again.

He kissed her head where new sprouts of blonde hair were forming. She had tried a wig, but it was very itchy and bothered her to the point that she finally donated it to the cancer wing of Maxwell University Hospital.

Peter had promised her that if anything, it was a wonderful reminder to him that he had one tough girlfriend and that she was alive because she was a fighter. He was very proud to call Ellen his girlfriend and now his fiancée.

"After graduation, right?" Ellen asked as she twisted the ring to shine in the spring sunlight again.

"Of course, after graduation," Peter agreed.

They packed up a few bags and headed home to Oakdale for a surprise visit. Ellen just couldn't wait to show her mom the beautiful ring and this kind of announcement had to be done in person. A phone call just wouldn't work.

When they arrived home late that evening, Betsy and Harold stepped out onto the porch. Realizing it was their daughter, they yelled inside for Daniel and Gaige.

When Ellen rose from the car, she held up her hand towards her mom. Betsy cried and held Ellen. Harold shook hands with his future son-in-law. Even Daniel and Gaige were happy for Ellen. They loved Peter, too.

They would set a date after graduation. But for now, they were happy just being together.

The family sat down together and held hands as Harold said grace over a delicious meal. Their laughter could be heard two houses down, but no one cared. They were safe, healthy, and happy. And they were together.

The End

Epilogue

The weather was perfect. The sun had shown all day and the heat beating down felt wonderful.

Somewhere in the distance, a radio blasted the soothing sounds of Jimmy Buffet. The waves were crashing down on the beach in Cancun.

Children were squealing with delight as the waves tickled and teased their ankles. Mothers and fathers were talking about stuff that didn't matter.

A cabana boy knelt down and offered a drink. He nodded with delight as he sipped the margarita made especially for him. *These are the days*, he thought to himself.

He was lazing away another day in paradise when he saw her. She walked by wearing a big rimmed, floppy hat and smiling a white flash of teeth. The sun had browned her skin to a perfect tan. She wore a long, red sundress. She couldn't have looked more dazzling.

Freddy stood and followed behind her several steps. He could feel the excitement growing as he stepped in the tiny footprints she made in the sand.

Well, shit, Fredlee. She is perfect, ain't she?

He touched her shoulder and she spun around, still smiling.

"Lori? I've missed you!"

About the Author

This story is very different from my first two novels and doesn't feature ghosts. I wanted to expand my writing and give my readers something different. Writing this was a fun adventure, due mostly to my own sick imagination. I do have a fascination with the undead, or ghosts, if you will, and love learning about them. As you have seen when reading this novel, I believe we all have a story to tell and a dark side that can be explored. If you've enjoyed it, watch for Two Grave Mistakes, which will be available in the fall of 2014.

Besides writing, I love spending time with my family, teaching my homeschool children and the youth at my church, as well as crafting and plundering in other people's junk. Yard sales and thrifting are a passion of mine.

Thank you for reading and I hope you enjoy!

Cindy

Follow Cindy

Facebook:
www.facebook.com/authorcindypondsnewell

Amazon:
www.amazon.com/author/cindypondsnewell

Goodreads:
www.goodreads.com/author/show/6490873

If you enjoyed *One Grave Secret*, please check out *Don't Say Her Name* and *The Kept: A Ghost Story*, available on Amazon.